HOW NOT TO
DROWN
IN A
GLASS OF WATER

Angie Cruz

JOHN MURRAY

First published in the United States of America in 2022 by Flatiron Books
First published in Great Britain in 2023 by John Murray (Publishers)
An Hachette UK company

1

A CIP catalogue record for this title is available from the British Library

Hardback ISBN 9781399806893
eBook ISBN 9781399806923

Printed and bound in Great Britain by Clays Ltd, Elcograf S.p.A.

John Murray policy is to use papers that are natural, renewable and
recyclable products and made from wood grown in sustainable forests.
The logging and manufacturing processes are expected to conform
to the environmental regulations of the country of origin.

John Murray (Publishers)
Carmelite House
50 Victoria Embankment
London EC4Y 0DZ

www.johnmurraypress.co.uk

Please return/renew this item by the last date shown. Books may also be renewed by phone or internet.

🖥 www.rbwm.gov.uk/home/leisure-and-culture/libraries

☎ 01628 796969 (library hours)

☎ 0303 123 0035 (24 hours)

www.rbwm.gov.uk

Royal Borough
of Windsor &
Maidenhead

ALSO BY ANGIE CRUZ

Dominicana

Let It Rain Coffee

Soledad

*Para las madres, tías, vecinas y comadres who know how
to resolver and take care of nuestra comunidad. For
the ones who've experienced rechazo.*

HOW NOT TO
DROWN
IN A
GLASS OF WATER

SENIOR WORKFORCE PROGRAM

New York, United States

The Senior Workforce Program is designed to provide career counseling, job listings, and similar employment-related services. All participants receive extended unemployment benefits for the twelve weeks they participate in the program to subsidize prevocational training that includes communication skills, interviewing skills, and punctuality to prepare them to reenter the workforce.

The final report will assess if the participant is job ready or not.

The following are the twelve sessions and documents that may or may not have supported the final report and recommendations.

SESSION ONE

My name is Cara Romero, and I came to this country because my husband wanted to kill me. Don't look so shocked. You're the one who asked me to say something about myself.

Before we begin, can you permit me to have a glass of water? Ay, yes. Thank you. Why am I so nervous? I know, I know, we're just talking. And this water, is it from the bottle? Does it taste strange to you? No?

I've never done something like this before. I didn't think I was going to have to look for a job at this point of my life. La Profesora from La Escuelita said that you'll help me. You're dominicana, no? She said if you know a lot about me you can find me a job. Is that true? Ay, good, because I need a job. The factory closed in 2007, right before Christmas. Can you believe that? Almost two years I don't work.

In reality, El Obama has been very generous. After the factory closed, I received fifty-three checks, then El Obama gave me thirteen checks, then twenty more. Did he have a choice? No. There are no jobs—my factory left to Costa Rica! You know they're never coming back. And after these twelve weeks that I meet with you—I'll receive no more checks! Like my neighbor Lulú says, El Obama is good, but not God.

I'm lucky because I'm fifty-five years old—wait, did I say fifty-five? I'm fifty-six! I stopped counting. If I don't, I'll be in a coffin sooner than I'm ready. The point is that I qualify for your Senior Workforce Program. Me, a senior? I told Lulú I'll be a senior for the checks but not for the canas. Ha!

You want to know how I found out about La Escuelita? OK, I can tell you. One year ago we received this letter from the government that we must report to La Escuelita to take classes. If not, no more unemployment checks. I did not want to go to La Escuelita because it was far away in Harlem. So, in the first day, I paralyzed. I had to fight to get out of the bed. I sleep maybe one hour or two, almost nothing. I couldn't even drink my café that morning. It was like I forgot how to dress. Does that ever happen to you? When the easy is impossible? But you have to understand, I stopped working in the factory and for twelve months I only wore my inside clothes. My belts, my blazers, my dresses—lost in the closet.

Thank God for Lulú who came to get me that morning. I tell you, on the first day of La Escuelita, Lulú appeared in my apartment with banana bread she makes at home, with nuts and chocolate, warm from the oven and said, You have fifteen minutes.

I didn't want to make Lulú late, so I speed up. She knew I would never go to La Escuelita by myself. And for this I pay the price, because for the rest of my life she will say, What would you do without me?

But don't worry, I don't need Lulú to take me to work— I'm ready to confront life. Look, already I'm losing some weight so I can fit into my blazers. Don't you think I look good with this one? You like it? Of course you do.

I never wear brown. My color is black. With my black eyes and hair, black makes me look elegant. This brown blazer is Lulú's. She looks good in this color because she dyes her hair blond—well, it's more like anaranjado because she does it from the box. But the color still looks good on her because her skin is like a penny. Not like a brilliant penny, more like an old penny. And she's only fifty-four. I tell her to drink more water so she gets more glow. But she doesn't listen. She is also more fat than me. But that doesn't matter. We're all more fat since losing our jobs. Lulú more than me. In fact, this blazer doesn't fit her anymore, even when she wears the faja. She never takes off the faja. Never. Not even to sleep. OK, maybe sometimes to sleep. But even in the dreams she wants to look like a botella de Coca-Cola. But when I tried the blazer, you should've seen her face: arrugada. But it's OK—jealousy. I'm accustomed to it. I know I was born with sugar in my pockets.

I loved La Escuelita. It opened my mind a lot. But it's not easy. When we started, La Profesora said she could teach us to keep numbers. How to use the computer. Even to read and write English! Ha! I have been in this country twenty-five—wait, no, almost twenty-seven years. I speak English good. You understand me, right? OK. But to read and write English? ¡No me entra! How you say a word in English is not how you write it. Why is that? You laugh, but it's true.

I told La Profesora—she dresses like a teacher from the TV, with the blusa buttoned all the way up to her neck—I'm too old to learn.

No, Cara. If you apply yourself, you'll learn to write English. I promise you. You can even go to college.

Ha! I laughed so hard I peed in my panties. This is what happens to women who have their babies natural. I carry extra panties in my purse and never leave my house without a Kotex.

How many children do you have? ¿Cómo? What are you waiting for? You don't want to have children? Listen to me: Don't wait until you get too old.

Lulú says that a person is never too old to do anything, especially to study. She said our neighbor La Vieja Caridad can go to college if she wanted to.

She's ninety years old! It makes no sense.

But why not? Lulú says. In New York, a lot of old people go to college.

Imagine if I live until ninety like La Vieja Caridad. I could go to college and work for another twenty years in una oficina or something.

In the Dominican Republic it's not easy to progress, but in New York La Escuelita is making me think I can dream. I learned many new things. I even have an email now. Did you know that?

Lulú is LuLu175 and I am Carabonita.

Hola, Lulú. ¿Cómo estás? Soy yo, Cara.

Ding! The computer tells us we got email.

Hola, cabroncita! Soy yo, Lulú.

Ding!

It's Carabonita!

Ding!

I know, cabroncita.

Ding! Ding! Ding!

And now I get many emails. Most of them are from Alicia the Psychic. One day, when I looked for my horoscope, I found Alicia through a button: FREE PSYCHIC READING. Of course I clicked it. It was La Profesora who said that the best way to learn how to navigate the internet is if we explore our interests.

Dear Carabonita,
I am delighted to hear from you. I can see that you are anxious for news to unblock all the obstacles in your path. Open my invitation to learn more about what awaits. For a small fee . . .

Your loving friend,
Alicia

In the beginning, Lulú read them for me, but the emails kept coming every day, and so Lulú showed me how to translate the email from English to Spanish. So easy. *Click.*

I am enchanted to know about you.
I have news from your personal protector.

When I get that email, I swear to you, the lights on the ceiling went on and off like in a discoteca.

Alicia the Psychic wrote to me even though I never sent her money.

She's a robot! Lulú said.

Impossible, I said.

Every time I checked my email there was a message from Alicia the Psychic who told me she was losing sleep because my protectors were keeping her awake at night.

La Profesora said to be careful of scams. Email is full of them. She said people like us are the perfect target.

People like us?

I told her and Lulú that I know what is real and not. I am not a pendeja.

Tell me, you educated dominicana taking all those notes: What do you really think about me? You think there's hope for me? Ay, qué bueno.

When La Escuelita recomendó I join this program so I can do interview practice, I said, Interview for what? And La Profesora said, For *all* the jobs you'll try for! Ha! Between you and me, she's very positiva, so she's hard to trust. Be honest: Do you really believe there's a job for me? Really? I've never heard of people that find a job without a key.

The news said this country is in a crisis! Nobody has jobs. It's the most great recession since the Depression, when the people didn't have cars and still made pee in pots. Well, maybe our building had toilets, but you understand what I'm saying. La Vieja Caridad, who lives in my building, re-members. She came from the revolutionaries of Cuba, José Martí and all those people. They lived in New York before the telephone and the electricity. For sure, they had no toilets that flushed. Our building didn't exist. She says there were more trees than people.

Yesterday in the news, I saw a lawyer with two chil-dren and a wife, so desperate that he took a job in Wendy's around here—not even downtown. Things are bad. More bad than bad. It's just like in Santo Domingo: when there is no fresh bread, you eat casava. I never thought the banks in the United States would rob people. But now I see that this country is like that fisherman with fast hands on the beach who shows you the big fat fish, but when he cooks, he says it shrink.

My money situation? It's OK right now because I get El Obama checks, but the only people I know who are prepared for the crisis are my sister Ángela and her husband, Hernán. They saved money for many years to buy a house in Long Island. Hernán doesn't want to leave our building because he can walk to work in the hospital every day, but Ángela, she detests Washington Heights. Pero detests. So every weekend they go to look for houses.

Remember early in the nineties, when things were so bad that you could buy an apartment downtown for $100,000? Maybe you're too young to remember. What age do you have? Thirty-five? Forty?

Wait, I didn't mean to offend. Of course, you look like a teenager.

What I wanted to tell you is that in the past Ángela and I, every weekend, went to look for apartments to dream. Now she dreams with Hernán. But I remember seeing an apartment in the street Eighty or Eighty-one, in front of Riverside—you know, where the rich live? You couldn't put an entire bedroom set in those rooms, only a bed, maybe a queen, and one of those tall bureaus. But the windows looking to the trees: wow. In those days, there were so many apartments like that, cheap. Now that same apartment costs more than one million dollars. I'm serious. Look it up!

Ángela talks about those apartments like they're the man who got away. From the day she arrived to this country she was determined to leave Washington Heights. To do this she counted her money and calculated how many years it would take for the down payment. And when she met Hernán, she told him immediately the plan. She said, If you want to be with me, saving is a family project.

Every day for breakfast, they talk about their goal: a down payment for the house. With a yard. A room for each child. A porch for the swing. She writes the progress on the refrigerator. Every time they save $1,000, they buy a small cake from Carrot Top and celebrate with the children. That way, the children learn that dreams only become real with hard work and saving money.

Hernán and Ángela save $50 a week. That's $200 a month. And that's $2,400 a year. In ten years, they saved $24,000. And we think ten years is a long time. But look at me, I worked in that factory for twenty-five years. And my son, Fernando, has been gone for ten.

Why do you say sorry? Ay, no. My son is not dead. He abandoned me. Maybe one day, si Dios quiere, I will tell you about Fernando.

But what I was saying is that time passes in a blink. If I would've saved even $10 a week maybe I wouldn't be in so much trouble now. The little bit I put aside I sent to the banks in Santo Domingo. I converted my dollars to pesos because the interest was higher. Yes, of course you shake your head. It was stupid! What a mistake. Overnight, the change rate went from RD$13 for $1 to RD$45 for $1.

Talking to you makes me remember the days Ángela and I got along. Now I can't remember the last time we were in the same room without her getting angry with me.

How old is she? Ángela is fifteen years younger than me.

She's my sister and we look the same age, but she could be my daughter. Maybe that's why, like my son, Fernando, she thinks everything I say is wrong. For example, tell me you— was I wrong to say that we should relax Yadiresela's hair? That's my niece. It looks like a broom when I brush it. Ángela gave me a lecture about chemicals and the damage it will make. She told me not to brush the children's hair. But how do I get out the knots? The fury she puts on me could burn down a forest. So now I say nothing.

Do you have a sister? Oh good, so you understand. Sisters don't always get along. But even when we fight, we eat dinner together, like a religion. Always we are two apartments but one house.

She makes me pudín de pan. I tell her it's too sweet and then everything is OK. Food, I tell you, fixes things.

Yes, yes, I know. I am here to talk about getting a job.

But my point is I know how to save money too. When I was able to make a little extra, I saved. And when times were good, I always made extra, like in the winters when I did mandaos for La Vieja Caridad. Back then I helped her a little, now I help her every day, especially after she fell on the steps in front of our building because the super let the snow turn to ice. But listen to this, she didn't even think to sue the building. We all told her to do it. But she said, I'm my father's daughter, and then sang, Yo soy un hombre sincero, de donde crece la palma. Do you know that song? Yes? It's a good one.

La Vieja Caridad calls me and says, Cara, can you do me a favor and pick up something in the store? I would do it with pleasure for nothing, but she insists on giving me her money. She is good to give me her money because, without her even asking, I know what she needs. With the years we've known each other, she is like family. I clean her apartment. And not only on the tippy-tippy of things like the dust on the TV and the shelves. No. I get on my hands and knees and scrub the floors and clean the faucet and the drains. I organize her refrigerator so she can find everything easy. I put in order her forks, knives, and the spoons in the drawers. You know, small things that make a big difference in the life.

Toma, La Vieja Caridad says, and puts $20 in my hand.

No, no, I say to her. I don't need the money.

Take, take, we all need.

She folds my fingers around the money like I do with children. I tell you, her skin, so thin and soft, like she's never worked hard in her life.

We do the dance, you know?

She never had children. You don't find that strange? No husband, no children. All her life, she lived with her childhood friend. When they walked together, they held on to each other. They fought in public like husband and wife. But no one knows for sure because until her friend died, I had never stepped into that apartment. It's not my business. But it's strange, right?

You don't think so? Ha!

Her companion now is the dog. Ay, how she loves that Fidel! Feeds him comida orgánica, you hear me? Home-cooked food delivered frozen. If not, the dog makes poop in the wrong place. But the dog is tiny, the size of my purse, so it's no problem to clean the mess. But I prefer to take him outside to make poop.

Yes, I walk the dog. In the morning and in the night—even when it rains and when it snows—because to me it's not hygienic to poop in the house. I also don't want no dog stinking the apartment. It doesn't take more than ten minutes to walk the dog. Between us, when I walk him, it feels nice to feel the fresh air hit my face.

What did you say? Yes, of course I want to find a job, that's why I'm here!

Please write that down: Cara Romero wants to work.

What is a person without an occupation? Since I could walk, Mamá taught me how to take Papá's shirt, put it into a ball, and scrub the devil out of it with a bar of jabón de cuaba. If Ángela, Rafa, and me didn't work, they hit us. If we worked wrong, they hit us. If we tripped, they yelled. If we looked to them wrong, cocotazo. If we cried from the cocotazo, another cocotazo.

Ay, don't look to me like that, like you feel sorry for me. All of that made me strong, you know? I had to be strong because what waited for me in this life. ¡Uf!

Let me tell you this: compared to my parents, my husband, Ricardo, was good to me. In the beginning, we were happy. But even the moon and the honey go dark and rancid. And I tell you, if I stayed in Hato Mayor, I would be dead.

Wait. One second. Permit me to drink some water.

Yes, I'm OK.

Maybe you've lived long enough to understand what I'm going to tell you: My husband Ricardo hadn't touched me since my son was born. Two years! That's una vida entera for a woman like me. I mean, look at me, you think I look good now, but imagine me thirty-eight years younger with brilliant eyes and all my hair. But suddenly you look in the mirror, and time bites off your face. All those years to not be caressed by somebody made me a dead person.

And then, Cristián appeared.

When somebody looks at you—pero *really* looks at you—and takes your hand and slides their finger up your lifeline. It is impossible not to fall. And I fell. Even if my son was sleeping in the other room.

It was only one time. I thought, *Who will know?* But men talk when they drink, and the words travel. My husband lost his head.

One night, he went to the house where Cristián lived, carrying a machete the length of his arm. Cristián lived down the road in the big house with the gates and the fancy cars that came and went. He was a quiet man with a reputation of being good. He never made trouble for nobody. Cristián was asleep, I'm sure, and just like that, Ricardo cut off his leg. One clean chop.

My mother always said, Don't mess with a butcher. And Ricardo could kill and skin a goat in five seconds.

Believe me, when I heard the scream, I understood that I was in trouble. I got up and pulled Fernando out of the bed, packed whatever I could carry in a garbage bag, and ran. Thank God Mamá lived only one mile away. The night, so dark I couldn't even see my hands in front of me. Better that way. I don't even want to think about what else was out in that dirt road.

Have you been to the monte in Dominican Republic? Have you? No? Oh.

Well, imagine, my son crying against my chest. Me, trying to *shh* him so not to wake the dogs, the snakes, the rats, the pigs. Not a car in sight. How many women have disappeared walking on that road? But I had no time to be afraid of the night or what waited for me. Better the earth eat us both than me to return to Ricardo. Ese salvaje. He would kill me to end the humiliation he felt. Forget about the million women he had fucked—but the one time I do it, the *one* time. *Pfft!*

Ay, I could feel all my skin, all my life, exploding. I was afraid my mother was going to send me back to Ricardo. She had said it too many times, she couldn't feed one more mouth, forget about two. She later asked, Why did you get under another man?

Yes, I was lonely, but I knew then and I know now: I did it because I wanted to change my life. That's what we have to do. We step in the shit on purpose so we're forced to buy new shoes. You know what I'm saying?

Why do you look at me like that? What I'm feeling?

I don't know. I don't feel nothing.

I know, I know. All of this sounds like from a movie. But I tell you the truth—that night on the road a car came speeding. And because life is life, another car came from the other direction, and right in front of me they crashed. Head-on. Like two crushed cans. A man went flying through the window and his body fell to the ground like, *prá*! My son Fernando cried. I tried to look for the body, but even with the lights of the car, it was not enough. The other driver was not moving, a river of blood coming out of the head.

I yelled. But who could hear me? How many people have died this way?

I knew in that moment that if I stayed in Hato Mayor,

I might as well be left to die like those two men on the road. Who knows where they were speeding to that night. Maybe they were good men. But life was finished for them.

You look worried for me. Don't worry. I am OK.

Write that down: Cara Romero is strong.

Lulú always says that when someone asks me about mangoes I talk about yuca.

Next time, I promise we will talk about how you will find me a job.

I've said enough for today. Don't you think?

APPLICATION

THE JOB YOU WANT & CO.
Washington Heights, New York, NY

Please fill out all the sections below:

Applicant Name: Cara Romero
Address: Washington Heights, NYC
Email: carabonita@morirsonando.com
Date of Application: Spring 2009
Are you a citizen of the United States: No
If not, are you authorized to work in the U.S.? Yes

The oral interview is to assess the following:

1. Interest in attaining employment
2. Personal character
3. Judgment
4. Ability to plan and organize tasks to meet deadlines
5. Ability to develop alternative solutions to a problem
6. Ability to understand verbal instructions
7. Ability to be self-motivated, responsible, and dependable without close supervision
8. Ability to work smoothly with others and to complete a task
9. Ability to remain calm in an emergency
10. Ability to communicate effectively

JOB APPLICATION, CONT.

THE JOB YOU WANT & CO. is an equal opportunity employer. This application will not be used for limiting or excluding any applicant for employment on a basis prohibited by local, state, and federal law.

Education and Training

High School: The yellow house on the hill near the colmado.
Location: Calle Sin Nombre.
Year Graduated: I learned my numbers and letters. My teachers said I was the most intelligent.
Degree Earned: Survival.

College / University

Name: One that doesn't cost anything.
Location: I heard the school in the Bronx is good.
Year: Maybe one day, who knows?
Degree Earned: Lulú calls me La Doctora because I can smell the sickness.

Vocational School / Specialized Training

Name: Pastry school? I can cook, but the oven and I fight.
Location: Close to the apartment.
Year Graduated: Si Dios quiere.
Degree Earned: The best tasting Dominican cake in Washington Heights. It's not pretty, but eating it, you die dreaming.

Previous Employment

Employer Name: The factory of little lamps.

Job Title: Whatever job needs to be done.

Supervisor Name: The good one or the bad one?

Employer Address: You cross the George Washington Bridge.

Dates Employed: 1980–2006

Reason for Leaving: The factory left to Costa Rica.

Position(s) Applying for: All the positions available.

How did you hear about this position?
Neighbors, families, friends, La Escuelita.

What days are you available for work?
Every day.

What hours or shifts are you available for work?
All the hours. All the shifts. Except between 8 to 10 at night, because I see the telenovelas. And not before 7 in the morning because I need the sleep. After 10 at night, I am not so good. On Sundays, I like to clean and do laundry and visit Ángela and Hernán and the children. I have to come home by 5 to make the dinner. But yes, I am available all the hours.

If needed, are you available to work overtime?
You don't have to ask.

On what date can you start working if you are hired?
Yesterday.

Salary desired:
Suficiente to live. They paid me $11 per hour. I started with $3.35 in the factory. But without overtime it was not enough.

Personal reference and relationship:
Lucía (Lulú) Sánchez Peña. She's my neighbor. Mi comadre.
Like family. I would put my sister Ángela, but I can't predict
what she'll say about me.

**How many years have you known your personal
reference?**
A life.

Are you 18 years of age or older:
Unfortunately, yes. But I look like a teenager. Ha!

**Are you a U.S. citizen or approved to work in the
United States?**
What do you think?

**What document can you provide as proof of citizenship
or legal status:**
I have the papers.

**Will you consent to a mandatory controlled substance
test?**
What kind of person do you think I am? Do I look like a tecata
to you?

**Do you have any condition which would require job
accommodations?**
I have veins like rocks, up and down my legs. A job that
doesn't destroy me would be nice.

Have you ever committed a criminal offense?
Well . . . it depends.

(Note: No applicants will be denied employment solely on the
grounds of conviction of a criminal offense.)

SESSION TWO

You are so serious today. Yes, I know we have a lot of work to do, but first I will get myself some water if that is no problem for you. Yes? OK.

What's this paper? More questions?

What are your strengths?

Ha! Is this not clear to you already?

What are your weaknesses?

Pfft! This question is a trick? OK, OK. I will play the game with you.

What is my strength? Hmm . . . first let me put on lipstick. It helps me to think.

But in serious, strength? When you ask, my mind paralyzes.

Maybe sometimes I'm too strong. But a mother needs to be strong.

Like one time, when my son, Fernando, had thirteen years, he wanted to go outside to be with some tígueres from the street. Ángela was living with us. Recently arrived. It was nice to have her with us but she always gave me ojo when she saw me with the chancleta in my hand.

Fernando tried to leave the apartment, even after I said no. He was a head-size taller than me. He tried to get to the door, and when he saw I was standing in the middle, his nose flared out to here, and his eyebrows came together like this. So I pushed him away from the door. He fell back and hit his head on the wall.

There was no blood. He was OK—it was an accident. I just didn't want him to go outside. Those delinquents give the children money to deliver packages. It's my responsibility to keep him safe! Look at that boy Jorge in my building who was suspended from the university for selling the drugs. He was in one of the best schools in the country, maybe even the world.

But you know what Fernando did the next day? He told his teacher I pushed him and showed her the small bump in the back of his head—a mosquito bite. And the teacher gave a report of abuse to the authorities. Abuse! The next week they came to do an inspection in the apartment. They asked me many questions. They looked in the refrigerator to see if there was food. They looked in his room to see if he had sheets on the bed. But, of course, they saw that in my house Fernando had more than any children need.

I couldn't look at him. He broke my heart. I told him: You want to live in a house with strange people who take the money from the government to buy the drugs? Is that what you want?

No, Mami, I'm so sorry. He cried like a baby. He didn't think of the consequences.

Only a mother knows this suffering. If Ángela was not watching me, I would have taken the chancleta and given him a real pela.

Years later, when Fernando left and didn't come back, Ángela was very angry at me. She's wrong to say that it's my fault. She doesn't think I'm a good mother because she says that Fernando was afraid of me. But she doesn't understand.

I taught him what to do when the policía stopped him. If they ask him where's he going. Or what he's doing. Or where he's coming from. I told him not to yell or curse. To be polite and always show the hands. To take a breath and ask, am I under arrest? To ask, am I free to go? And under no circumstance, never, to walk away until the policía says it's OK to go.

Did your mother teach you this? No? You see, this is why I am a good mother. Because many mothers don't teach their children how to be with the policía and we have tragedies because of this. The policía do not take care of our children. *We* have to take care of them.

I told Fernando to stay far away from those chupacabras from the neighborhood. To use me like an excuse. Call me whatever name he wants—as long as everybody understood that my eyes were glued on him.

At least, when he was living with me, he never went to the prison. He never impregnated a girl. And he did good in the school. All of this is success to me.

And when Ángela and our brother Rafa arrived to New York with eyes shut and open mouths, I had to take care of them too. Ángela had twenty-five years, Rafa had thirty-two years. They were adults, but the sight of snow blinded them. For some years we lived together. We worked all of the time. They were my responsibility. But it was good because we were close and I think happy together.

After Rafa went to live with Miguelina, Ángela stayed with me. In those years, Ángela took Fernando to every place because she wanted to know New York. Fernando translated for her. To learn English they went together to many movies. I did everything possible so that Ángela could study and be a professional. I even worked Saturdays and Sundays sometimes. Two, even three jobs, so she could focus on getting the diploma.

Instead of buying something for me, I made sure my son and my sister had what they needed so they could progress. I was the one that registered Ángela for the program ESL. I was the one that helped her get the GED diploma. And from the day she landed in the Kennedy airport, I got the job for her in the factory so that she could make money. I helped Ángela to get an apartment in the building so Hernán could move with her and they could start their life together.

Did I think about *my* future? No. Do you think she remembers that it was me who saved her from some burro destroying her life? No. In Hato Mayor, there are no choices for women like us. So many of my primas have more children than I can count, with different fathers who contribute nothing. Without my sacrifice, Ángela wouldn't have all those diplomas in the wall. She wouldn't have all those fancy downtown friends. Now she walks around here with her nose pa'rriba.

Ay, I need some more water. Will you permit me to get some? Thank you.

Ever since the operation, I'm thirsty like never.

That's right, I had an operation a few days before our first meeting. Did you see I was dying from the pain that week? Of course you didn't. And did I cancel our meeting? No. Even when I feel like I'm dying from the pain, I keep my commitments.

Now you look horrified. Don't worry. I'm fine. I just had a cyst removed.

You see, a few months ago, I felt a pain in the left side. And I hadn't been to a doctor in a long time because I don't have the insurance. But when my friend Glendaliz got cancer in the colon, I had the feeling to get checked too. Because of me, Glendaliz was able to discover her cancer early. The cancer on her skin smelled like mangoes, the kind you find in the playa. They smell both salty and sweet. Even over the smell of the cake I made for Glendaliz's son—when she hugged me, all my little hairs on my arms stood up.

Yes, I have an incredible sense of smell. It's my friend and my enemy. Certain smells can give me a pain in the head that makes me walk around like the ceiling is falling on top of me. But what can I do? I have a nose like a dog. You see that bump right here? It looks like I broke it, but no, that's God's pinch.

When I was young I didn't understand why some human smells, the little smells that people don't sense, gave me a pain in the head. But now I understand. You wouldn't believe how many people I've saved or could have saved from big things if they had only listened to my nose.

So yes, when I felt the pain, I tried to wait until I secured the insurance. My insurance went away when the factory went away. But when I say I felt the pain, I couldn't wear anything without the elastic because my stomach was inflated. I couldn't wait anymore.

I found a doctor who said if I make the down payment I can pay every month a little bit. So I made the down payment and now I pay every month for the operation. But don't worry, I applied to see if El Obama will pay the bill for me. I hope.

The operation, the doctor said, was only going to take a few hours, and only a few days to recover. Most people would take many days off, but I came to see you anyways. And even if the doctor said somebody had to pick me up in the hospital, I told nobody about the cyst.

I did it all by myself. That's how incredible I am.

When the doctor asked if somebody was coming to pick me up, I said yes, that they will come to me soon.

My fingers were shaking like *this*. My legs too. The pain in my stomach. Ay, it hurt, you have no idea! More than I thought. But I collected my things to go home.

But this gringa nurse chased me. Miss! Miss! ¡Esperah! ¡Noh puede salida!

You can't tell me what to do, that's what I wanted to say.

The policy, the nurse said, swinging her ponytail like Fidel does his tail when I enter the apartment of La Vieja Caridad. The nurse told me to sit and wait or I vomit or faint.

Can I teléfono familia for you? she asked.

I'm fine thank you, I said, even if my stomach had me blind.

Lo sientoh, Ms. Romero, but you must be accompanyamente. Sienta in sala, she said.

Bathroom, please?

She showed me where the bathroom was. Next to the exit. When she turned her back to me, I escaped and got in a taxi.

Look, I'm not someone to bother people. No way. Everyone is busy with their problems. They can't take time off to pick me up from the hospital. So I don't bother people.

Everything hurt, but I left that hospital with my head high.

That poor taxi driver was so worried about me.

He asked, Where to?

I swear to you, I couldn't remember where I lived. My mind went to zero.

Miss, you OK?

Fort Washington, I said.

I had to fight to not vomit. Everything made me feel sick.

The vibration of the car. The smell of the seats. I felt so bad. Ay, Dios mío. I vomited on the seat and on the glass between the driver and me. But fortunately I hadn't eaten anything that day so the mess was not big.

Miss! Miss!

He tried to stop the car but there was a lot of traffic. Because I am strong, I reached to open both windows to get some air. And the cold air felt good. Then I cleaned up my mess. In my bag I always have napkins, the dry ones and the wet ones. I even carry plastic bags for emergencies like this.

Write that down: Cara Romero is always prepared.

I take you back to the hospital, he said.

No, I'm fine, I said.

I park. I help you, OK?

No, please. Fort Washington.

That doesn't happen every day, you know? A person you don't know, with his own problems, offering to help? When we arrived in my building, he got out of the car to open the door. I stepped out of the taxi and, with all the strength left in me, stood up. And I smiled. Like I told you, I'd rather die than bother a person. I gave him a good tip. When he looked in the back seat, I could tell he was impressed. There was no sign of me left in the car.

I cannot tell you how I walked up the stairs. Of course, the elevator was broken that day. That night I told La Vieja Caridad I could not make her dinner or walk Fidel. The next day, Hernán came for a coffee and he talked and talked and I listened to him complain about his job in the hospital. Ángela brought some food that was going bad in the refrigerator. But did she notice my condition? Of course not. Her eyes always in the mirror. The phone always in the hand.

Lulú did notice that I took very little sips of the wine. That nothing was cooking on the stove. That the window in the kitchen was closed. I always leave it open, even on the most cold days, because I have a fire burning inside of me. But that day I was cold in the bones.

What do you have? she asked.

I'm just tired, I said.

I don't need people saying to me that everything will be OK. Of course I'll be OK. What other choice do I have? Who has the luxury of having someone to take care of them? Maybe only my sister Ángela, who married a man like Hernán.

Let me give you some advice, fall for the man who loves you more than you love him.

Do you have a good man in your life? No? You should secure someone while you are still young. Ángela did this and look how good she has it. Hernán takes care of everything. The food, the children, and her.

It's not so easy to find a good companion. In this age, not so easy. I prefer to be alone than in bad company. So if I can do things on my own, I do.

Lulú understands me. Hours later, she brought me a sopa de pollo, with arroz, not fideos, the way I like it. And a big thermos of tea made with ginger, turmeric, garlic, and honey.

If I had told Lulú that I had gone to get the operation without saying anything to her, she'd be angry.

But she's the same like me. Three years ago, she had a pain in the tooth that had her chewing only on one side. Maybe she could trick everybody else, but not me. This pain lasted for weeks. She could not get the root canal fast because she didn't have insurance and had to save money to pay for it. I, too, had pain in the teeth. But I went to the dentist to fix it, even if now I pay every month a little bit, because I don't want to be old without teeth.

Lucky for her I know many remedios. I froze some bags of té de menta so she can put it in her mouth to help the pain go away. When I took them to her, her son Adonis was sitting in the kitchen. Lulú was serving him a steak, because that's what he likes.

Are you OK, Mami? Adonis asked.

You know what she did? She took a bite of the steak and chewed. She even smiled. I know que esa vaina hurt like the devil.

Ay, now it's me that is too serious. This is why I prefer not to talk, because if you don't talk, it is more easy to forget the things of life.

Can you permit me to get myself another glass of water? These cups are so small.

Something I like to do? OK, I will tell you.

Every night, Lulú comes over with two glasses of wine—not the full bottle, because Lulú likes to save the wine. She loves the wine. Some days, we sit for hours and watch the camera in the lobby. Ever since those people who can pay two times the rent moved in a few years ago, the management, who's like *this* with the policía, installed a camera that watches the door of the building. If we turn the TV to Channel 15, we can see who comes and goes twenty-four hours a day.

In truth, when there is no novela to watch, it's how we entertain ourselves. Because we can't sit outside to get some fresh air with the radio on like we used to. We were out there so much, we chained our chairs to the stairs in the lobby. The old super who lived in the basement would bring out the barbecue. We'd throw chicken, hamburger, everything we wanted on it. And the management never said nothing. But now, dique everything is a fire hazard.

We were able to do what we wanted before the hospital opened all the laboratories and those other people moved in. And it's good that now the management doesn't let the elevator stay broken for weeks and the lobby has a painting of some mountains hanging on the wall. They even put some plants in the hallway—they're false, but it looks fancy. But now the policía gives you a ticket if you sit outside or turn up your radio. Can you believe that? The point is, they want us out, like we weren't here first.

I don't care that nothing happens on Channel 15. I leave it on all day. Sometimes the boy from 2F turns the camera to face the wall so he can sell in the lobby. Not *drug* drugs, but pain pills that he buys from las viejas in the building who have the Medicaid. I took one of those pills many years ago, when I had the pain on my back from working in the factory. I couldn't stand up. The doctor insisted to try them. You know what? That little pill emptied me. For one day I didn't think about my son Fernando. All my suffering, erased. It was the devil, I tell you. I threw them in the garbage.

Channel 15 gets interesting when people come home. I see my neighbor Tita and her daughter Cecilia—she never developed, and for the twenty-something years that I've known Cecilia, she's been in a wheelchair. I see Fedora and her big hair always carrying some box. I even caught my sister Ángela and Hernán holding hands—at their age. Can you believe it?

When I see La Vieja Caridad in the lobby on Channel 15, I go down to help her. She can only walk with the cane now.

Ay, to be old and have to wait for help. All she wants is to stand outside and get the sun. I put on my shoes and a little bit of lipstick to go help her. But when I arrive, someone's already opening the door. It's OK, I can always use ten minutes of sun. I go and stand outside with La Vieja Caridad. We know: the secret to a long life is to get at least ten minutes of sun every day.

Yes, that could be a good job for me. I could take care of old people. I know what they need before *they* know what they need.

For example, I told La Vieja Caridad to get checked for the blood because I could smell something was not correct. Also, I see her eyes go far away in the distance más y más, like she's looking over my shoulder. When that happens, I take her to her apartment and make her the green tea with honey, because, you know, the tea helps to focus. When I went through the menopausia, I was forgetting phone numbers and the names of things. Lulú told me to drink the green tea. Every day we drink two cups to maintain the mind. You know?

But anyways, Lulú and I noticed more strange people coming and going. And not strange like it was many years ago, when 3H was of the drugs. No, mostly young people from who knows where, with suitcases and backpacks.

If we, who have been in this building for decades, rent our apartments to other people, it's dique illegal, but *these* new people that pay double the price make this building like a motel. We don't rent rooms to strange people who come and go. We rent to someone of confidence for months. For example: Pargat Singh. He was such a nice young man. Many years ago when I needed money, I rented the room of my son

Fernando. Trust me, this was not easy to do because I had been saving his room for years exactly like he left it, waiting for him to return. Always, I put a plate for Fernando on the table when I ate. Always, I hung a clean towel for Fernando on the bathroom door.

But the point I'm trying to make is that I rented a room to Pargat, who came from las Indias to work in the hospital. He loved living with me because he could go in and out of the laboratory at all hours to check his experiments. He was alone, without family. Because I didn't let him to use the kitchen, every time I cooked, I gave him to eat. In the beginning, he didn't eat, to be polite. But then he got comfortable and ate. Still today, when he is in the neighborhood, he brings me pan dulce or some little thing and says hello.

These other strange people who come in and out of the building, what do they bring? Bedbugs and criminals. I tell you—crime is up like never.

This is more reason why Lulú and I have to be like guards. Except that, for the past few days, Lulú has abandoned her post. Last week we were in my apartment and her son Adonis appeared on Channel 15. He was in the entrance, but he did not ring the door. It was like he forgot the number of the apartment of his own mother.

Cara, open the door! Lulú yelled.

I pushed the button to let him in. We saw him enter the lobby and walk to the elevator.

Lulú, like a chicken without a head, ran down to her apartment to wait for her prince. But when Lulú left, I saw Adonis walk in and out of the camera, in and out. But he didn't go up. He left the building.

That was so strange. Why travel all the way from Brooklyn to just stand in the lobby?

Pobrecita Lulú. After, she emptied like a broken balloon in my kitchen table.

I said, Let me make you un café. Maybe he'll come back.

I was trying not to show that I was a little bit happy. Ay, yes. It's so bad, but I was a little bit happy. Finally, she could feel the misery of a son abandoning his mother. I hope you don't think I'm a bad person. I love Lulú. I do. I never make something in my kitchen without putting something on the side for Lulú.

When did we meet? *¡Uf!* Everybody knows everybody in the building. But Lulú and I didn't really *know* each other. We worked all the time. But we shared a tube that runs from the ceiling through the floor in our kitchens. We can hear everything that happens through that tube of metal. When the children still lived with her, the fights, ay, the fights. Of what? I don't know. She pretends her children are perfect. I know the reality.

She thinks that because her son went to the good school and has the bank job, he'll take care of her when she gets old. Good for her; I want good things for Lulú. But really? Why can't she keep all that inside her mouth? She knows I can't count on Fernando to take care of me.

Lulú has a daughter too: Antonia. She never visits. She studies and studies and studies. Has a mountain of diplomas. And guess what? She doesn't even have a job with benefits. She writes poems. All about Lulú. And not very nice ones. Antonia wrote a book and dedicated it to her mother—after all, Lulú

did raise her, with no help from the father. But now Antonia spits on her mother. That's what therapists make you
do. They make you spit on your mother. Everything is the
mother's fault.

Look, if Lulú had not been strong with her daughter she
would have baby with some atrabanco. She would have never
gone to the college and could never write that poem that
supposedly won her a $1,000 prize. One thousand dollars!
She should be publishing a thank you letter to her mother's
chancleta. It saved her life!

I bet Fernando went to therapy. I bet he spits on me.

Do you go to therapy? Yes. Ah. Interesting. Do you spit
on your mother?

Ay, I'm sorry. No, no I don't need more water. But thank
you.

Lulú and I became friends after my son Fernando left.
I was a disaster. I stayed in bed, forgetting to eat, to bathe,
to brush my hair. You know the rag that we use to mop the
floors? Stained, with holes and loose threads? That was me
when Lulú became my friend.

One day, I opened the door of the elevator and she was
there. You know when someone shocks you like a ghost? My
purse flew up and my lipstick, my change, my Kleenex, my
wallet, my keys, my aspirins, my banana for when I got hungry, all the photos of my son that I carried for when I asked
strangers if they had seen him—all of that fell to the floor.

Sorry! Sorry! I was saying, because I couldn't gather my
things, which is something not normal for a Capricorn.
Capricorns are solid like a tree. But I was so lost without
Fernando.

Do you need help? ¿Un café? Lulú asked.

Imagine me, on the floor, looking up to Lulú with her big orange hair. I did want un café. I didn't want to return to my empty apartment. The neighbors said Lulú thought she was better than other people because, like I told you, her son went to the fancy college and her daughter was a writer. But that day she was very nice to me. And because Lulú's not organized like me, and I like to stay occupied, while she made the café I took the broom and swept her floor. Then I saw a photo of Adonis on Lulú's wall, and I became a fountain.

Lulú gave me a box of Kleenex. She turned on the radio. She turned on the stove to make me dinner and told me that I can stay there as long as I needed, para desahogarme.

You never heard that word? You said you're dominicana. You don't understand Spanish? Oh, just a little. OK. Desahogar: to undrown, to cry until you don't need to cry no more.

Anyway, when Fernando left, Lulú did something for me that not even my sister Ángela would do. When Ángela saw me cry, my sister said, You're drowning in a glass of water.

I tell you, Ángela is cold. But cold! *Pfft!* She has no feelings for me.

Not Lulú. She understood that I had to cry until I undrowned from the inside.

I see you're taking notes. So many notes. It's true, you can write a book about me, because what I've lived has a hundred chapters.

In truth, all this, being here, with you, talking so much, it has taken me by surprise. I don't like to talk about my problems. People talk and talk and talk and I say nothing. Punto final.

Will you permit me to take a break?

Oh, I see, we have finished time.

Does your bathroom have a mirror?

NEW YORK STATE

Unemployment Insurance Benefits
Department of Labor

User Name: carabonita
Email: carabonita@morirsonando.com
Password: Fernando1980@@

Welcome carabonita

What is your maternal grandmother's maiden name?
Nobody remembers. We called her Mona because when she
was still married with Abuelo, dique she fell in love with a
Haitian who traveled to Paris to do the business and died on
the plane or the train or in the car. The story is always different. This Haitian went crazy over Abuela's smile. He gave
money to some artista to paint her face on the side of the store
in Hato Mayor. The mural is still there. You can't see it well,
but still. We called it la Mona Linda. Do you know the painting? Very famous. Look, if the Haitian hadn't died, Abuelo
would have chopped off his leg. Abuelo was not an easy man.
But did I learn? No. I married Ricardo anyway.

What is your favorite TV show?
Sin senos no hay paraíso. Everybody loves that show.

What is your favorite vegetable or fruit?
Mamey, especially in a batido. But if someone cuts it for you,
it's better.

What was the name of your first pet?
Pet? I don't know how Americans have animals inside the
house. I don't make opinions. I like La Vieja Caridad's dog,
Fidel. But she lets the dog eat from the spoon! It's not hygienic.

What is the first name of your childhood best friend?
My mother doesn't believe in friends.

**What was your childhood phone number including area
code?**
We had to go to the colmado to call people. I don't remember
the number.

Who was your first employer?
La abogada gave me a job to *supposedly* clean the house when
I had twelve or thirteen years. Instead, she made me fix the
husband's nails and sacarle caspa. Some lawyer she was.

What is your spouse's mother's maiden name?
Call her La Virgen María. It's a miracle Ricardo was even
born.

What was the first concert you ever attended?
Ay, José Luis Perales. You know the song? Y cómo es él . . . En
qué lugar se enamoró de ti . . .

**What subject or class did you dislike the most in
school?**
I learn everything possible. You stay ignorant or you educate.
Punto.

**What was your favorite comic book/cartoon character
as a child?**
Books? Cartoons? Child? Ha! We were never children.

What band poster did you have on a wall when you were in high school?

It's true that the Americans don't have any idea of what life is for us.

SESSION THREE

Ay, sorry I am late. Please forgive me. Don't think that late is something I do.

Yes, I am feeling fine. Until you said something, I forgot about the surgery. When did that happen? Three weeks ago?

The reason I'm late is because Lulú did not appear. You have to understand; I'm a Capricorn, and when a Capricorn gets in a routine, it takes an earthquake to move them. Every day, Lulú comes to my apartment to drink un café, because I make it better. So when Lulú didn't appear today, I lost my understanding of the day.

For ten years, Lulú and I took the bus to the factory together. Every day. Then, when that was finished, we went to La Escuelita together, all the way in Harlem. And now, even if La Escuelita is finished, she still comes to my apartment every morning and we talk about our dreams. No, not the dreams we make for the future, but dreams from when we sleep and get information about our life. Sometimes we don't know what is happening in us, but the dreams know. So we must listen. They can be like messages from something more big than us. Lulú needs my help to interpret the dreams so she can choose the numbers she plays on Sundays.

It doesn't hurt to try, that's her lotto motto. Ha!

She loses a few dollars every week, but she wins money too. Don't worry. I already warned her that playing the numbers is a dangerous game when you don't have a job.

Between us, my dreams are more interesting than Lulú's.

She dreams of the teeth falling out of the mouth. Very normal for people to dream that. I had a dream where my bed becomes a boat, then I am on the water and I see this man and he turned to me. It was Fernando. I tried to reach him, but the more close I got, the more far he went. I woke up with my shirt wet from sudor.

I know, I know, I'm not here to talk about Lulú. But I'm worried about Lulú. How can I think about jobs? This morning, Lulú didn't appear—and she didn't answer the phone. In fact, all weekend she was dique occupied. She didn't say with what, but ever since we saw her son Adonis on Channel 15, Lulú has been avoiding me. I am worried because she has never done anything like this before.

Listen, it's not easy to be a mother.

Everybody around the area uses Adonis like a good example when they talk to their children. His diplomas and certificates hang on the entrance in Lulú's apartment. They're framed, even the ones from elementary school. *Best Reader! Perfect Attendance!* Adonis came out blanquito, with good hair, and you can't tell me that didn't help his grades in school. And yet, I noticed from my window that when he was a boy, Lulú would hold the back of his neck, tight, like she was driving him. A mother knows when the pineapple is sour.

Who can blame her? The streets wanted boys like Adonis. They wanted my son Fernando too, so we held on tight. And Lulú knew Adonis loved the money. For sure, selling drugs would send him to jail. But those men from the banks who ruined everybody's lives and made people lose their houses— nobody is locking them up. *Pfft!* So I give it to Lulú. She managed to raise a son who is very successful.

Between you and me, Adonis is especial. She never said no

to him, and made un monstruo. A baby with mocos in his nose acting like a prince. Everything Adonis wanted, Lulú gave to him. She raised him to think the world was going to do the same.

I was strong with Fernando. I told Lulú we have to be mother and father to the children, and that means saying no. I had to say, no y no y no many times to Fernando, but it's because he was different than the other boys. In the school, when he was little, the children took everything from him and he did not fight. I got upset because in this life if we are not careful people take advantage of us. I had to be strong because I didn't want him to end up being . . . you know. Different.

How can I explain? Have you ever been dancing? There was a time Lulú and I went to dance in El Deportivo almost every Friday night. For this occasion I put on the makeup and nice clothes. And because I dance like a feather, I never sat down. You know the song by Los Hermanos Rosario that goes: Esa muchacha sí que baila bueno—they wrote that song for me. ¡Ay, sí! Men always chose me, even above the women who were young and dressed cheap like a cup of flour. When I went to dance, I forgot my life.

I enjoyed the feeling to be touched on my back in just the right way. In my experience, not every man knows how to hold a woman. Their hands, too high on the back, like they don't know themselves. There's no place for a man like that on the dance floor. A man without direction. And the worst is to be trapped with someone like that when the song takes forever. You can't stop in the middle of the song. It's too embarrassing for them. But these men are not free. They are soft.

I didn't want that for Fernando.

When he was still a teenager, we had a big party for Christmas. All the building came to our house. I made a lot of food. Rafa was the DJ. We danced until three in the morning; that does not happen no more. That night Hernán brought his primo Elvis to the party. He was visiting from the Dominican Republic and he was different.

You know, different, like *soft*.

The bottle of coñac and all the Presidentes were finished. The walls were wet con sudor. All of us, flying from the drinking. The music on full volume. The TV on mute. The Christmas lights on and off, on and off. The presents, opened.

And I couldn't find Fernando.

Fernando! I yelled on top of the music. And then I saw him, separating from Elvis—the feet moving one direction, the eyes the other.

I took his arm and pulled him to me. He smelled different: less vanilla, more Clorox. I don't know what I saw, but I am a mother. Something was changed in Fernando's face. His dark sleepy eyes, more open. You know when the eyes tell stories? And Elvis was dancing como un loco in his guayabera and tight pants. I knew Fernando was holding a secret in his mouth. I never saw the baby in his eyes again.

Later Hernán told me that Elvis had been in a fight in school, more than one time, for being with another boy. For *being* with another boy. You understand?

After that night, I could not stop thinking if only that day wouldn't have happen, maybe my Fernando would have been normal. I worried all the time about people taking advantage of him. I was afraid that he was like that, soft. I wanted him to have an easy life. Simple. So I fight extra to make sure he's strong.

One time, when I sent him to pick up a radio from the casa of Rafa, only one block away, some delinquents steal it from him. I saw it happen from my window. Two boys, more tall than him, took the radio from his hands in the middle of the day, not even at night. He practically gave it to them.

When he came home, I asked, What's wrong with you?

He walked away from me, went to his room, and tried to close the door.

But I didn't let him.

Look at me, I'm talking to you. Why are you such a pendejo? I saw what happened.

I talked and I talked and he didn't say nothing. He looked at his feet. To the floor, to the window.

Didn't I teach you to defend yourself?

He looked everywhere but at me. His bottom lip like a fruit low on a tree.

Ah, pendejo? Answer me!

What? No, that's not when he abandoned me. That was later, in 1998. This was a different fight.

You know, I never stopped looking for Fernando.

Everybody else gave up looking, but not me. And not Hernán. He has a spot in his heart for me. This drives my sister Ángela crazy.

You're my husband, not hers! Ángela throws me in his face when they fight.

When we were children, if somebody brought us chocolate, Ángela would hide it so that she can eat it all by herself. More than one time, the mice discovered it first. And guess what, then nobody ate the chocolate.

This is why Hernán doesn't tell her when he visits me.

Don't look at me like that. He comes to my apartment to take a break from his life and from her. We watch the Turkish telenovelas together and talk tonterías, nothing more.

But wait, before we talk about these questions you want me to answer, I want to tell you this story!

So, like I was saying to you, Hernán never stopped looking for Fernando. And because he works in the hospital he knows everybody. Somebody who knows somebody who knows somebody gave him the address for Fernando in September of 2001.

Remember that time? How old you were? Twenty years? So yes, of course you do. Who could forget? The entire world saw the fire in the sky. I could not sleep thinking that we were in a war and I was going to die without seeing my son in flesh and bone.

Hernán gave me the address thinking I would sleep better if I knew he had a place to live. But it was the opposite. Once I had the address, I could think of nothing else.

What kind of mother would stay away from her children?

Hernán said, Write to him. Tell him he should come home.

Even Lulú was against me going to Fernando. She said if I go after him he will run.

Lulú reads many magazines. According to the magazines if I focus on my life, stop thinking about things I can't control, maybe like a good ending to a telenovela, Fernando will knock on the door, with flowers. Maybe grandchildren. Maybe a lotto ticket full of money.

I don't know. Who are the people that write in these magazines? Not people like us.

Between you and me, it's a mystery that Fernando has not

come back in all these years. I don't understand how he survived without me. When he left he had a job in the place for
donuts downtown, but it paid him nothing. Life is expensive.

So when the city became more calm, I took a taxi to the address Hernán gave me in the Bronx. The lobby door, with no
lock. Brown stains on the walls. The stairs, dark. A strange
smell—it made me dizzy.

I knocked on the door 4H, checking Hernán's writing of
the address on the paper.

I heard the TV. I knocked again, hard. All I wanted was
to take my son with me.

Fernando! I yelled through the door. It was late. People
had to work the next day. But this was my chance. Fernando!

Then, a flaco man opened the door. He was wearing a
transparent shirt, gold earrings, and makeup in the eyes. My
heart fell to the floor. Maybe Hernán gave me the wrong address. This flaco, friends with *my son*?

I am Fernando's mother, I said.

Umm . . . he's not here? he said.

He lives here, right? I checked the address in my hand.
Where is my son?

Look, you should go home, el flaco said. It's late.

Fernando! I yelled even when he closed the door in my
face. I knew he was there, so I was ringing and ringing the
bell until some viejo came out of another apartment to yell
to me for making noise.

Did I return? Of course. I was very hurt, but a mother
does not give up.

The building was less bad than I remembered. The floors
were shiny and smelled like Fabuloso, not stinky like before.

No ice cream papers pushed into the corners. Maybe the super cleaned it? I knocked again on 4H. No one answered.

Of course, I waited. The trip was not cheap. Eventually, everybody has to come home. I waited more than one hour. I waited even if every bone in my body hurt from working all day in the factory with those machines—up and down, up and down. *Clamp. Clamp. Clamp.* Look at my leg. This is the price of all those years working with the machines. Look. Look! See the veins? Like mountains. I should've sued that factory for what they did to my legs. Back in the day, these legs stopped traffic. When I put on the dress and the heels, ¡Ay, papá!

Ángela says it's the inflammation. That I have to stop eating the milk, the pasta, the bread, the sugar, and the pain will go away. This is why Ángela looks like un palo. She does not eat. It's a problem. The doctor said if I lose ten pounds, it will feel like one hundred pounds less for my knees. He told me I should exercise every day. But I don't have time for that. What's a little pain?

So yes, I waited a long time in the stairs of Fernando's building. Every time I heard the elevator go to the fourth floor, my heart stopped. Una vieja thought I was going to rob her when I jumped up to help her with the door. But pobre vieja, her hair was like a nest on the back of her head. Why be alive if you don't have somebody to brush your hair? Even the viejas locas in Hato Mayor have their people. In this way, New York is very difficult. In Hato Mayor, Fernando would never have left, because where would he go? When you need each other to survive, you forgive. That's the way it is.

I was about to give up, but el flaco with the transparent shirt came out of the elevator. This time, he was wearing a furry coat and the hair was blue. Like he belonged in the future.

He dropped the bags he was carrying. The botella de olivas broke and made a big mess on the floor.

What's wrong with you? he said.

Ay, I'm so sorry, I said and tried to help him.

It's OK. Don't worry, he said, and opened the door of the apartment.

Then he recognized me.

Wait a minute. You're that lady that showed up last week?

I want to see Fernando, I said.

El flaco tried to close the door, but I'm strong. I pushed my body against it to keep it open. I put my foot in the way.

He's not here, he said.

He pushed one way. I pushed the other.

I don't believe you, I said.

Fernando doesn't want to see you, he said.

But the world is going to finish! He has to see his mother one more time before we all die from the terroristas, I said. But then I thought maybe el flaco was saying the truth. I let go of the door. The fountain again. So much crying. So much mocos came out of my nose. I had to use the sleeve of my shirt, like a child.

Fine. Come in. I'll get you a Kleenex, el flaco said. Can't be crying out here. I don't want you to make the building sad.

I took small steps. I knew I was inside Fernando's house, even if I recognized nothing. In the sala there was no sofá, only big pillows in the floor around the table with the shape of an egg. Little lights around the windows. A radio in the corner.

El flaco cleaned the floor in the hallway and then went from one end of the room to the other like a bird trapped inside the apartment. He looked at me cry until I could breathe again.

All this was my grandmother's, he said. She died on that chair and left the apartment and everything in it to me. I'll make you café. OK?

In the apartment I saw a big photo of Walter Mercado. The photo remind me how every night, all of us, Ángela, Fernando, Lulú, and I would wait to listen to Walter's horoscopes.

To be different is a gift, it said under Walter's face.

And what Walter says is siempre correct but to be raro like el flaco is not a gift—it's a life of suffering. You understand what I say?

Of course you don't. You are American. Anyway, I asked his name and when he said, Alexis . . . Ay, Dios mío, out of all the names he could say—do you know Alexis is the protector of all humanity?

The café came fast. Alexis moved in the kitchen like he had never been in it before. Three jars of adobos and no sugar in the cabinets.

I asked him, Do you know where my Fernando is?

Sorry, Mami, he said, I hope you can drink café like that.

I pointed to the photo of Walter Mercado. I am a Capricorn, I said.

My grandmother was a Capricorn!

She must have been a great woman. Capricorn is the best sign. We are loyal and we never give up, I said. You can tell that to Fernando.

Then I asked, What is your sign? And he said, I am a
Pisces, like Walter.

Could you believe it? He is a Pisces. And everybody
knows Pisces is full of corazón.

When I finished drinking the coffee, I asked if Fernando
talked about me.

He misses your cooking, Alexis said.

Of course he does. I am the best cook in Washington
Heights.

He laughed. And then I laughed—I tell you, I felt this
relief in the chest.

Then Alexis looked to me very serious and said, Listen to
me, if you come here again, Fernando will leave. I don't want
him to leave. Do you understand?

I took another sip because I didn't understand—am I so
terrible that he have to run away from me?

I don't know why, maybe it was Walter Mercado that
gave me the message, but I trusted what El flaco Alexis the
Pisces was saying to me. So I told him I will stay away under
one condition: if something happened to Fernando he must
contact me immediately. I left him my address and phone
number.

The next day, I put my electric bill in Fernando's name
and made the process to put his name on the lease of the
apartment. If something happens to me, Dios no lo quiera, I
can do this for him. I also ordered him delivery from his favorite Dominican restaurant: pernil with white rice and tostones
with garlic on the side. The note said, Fernando, te quiero. Tu
mamá.

He didn't call to say thank you.

But at least then I knew he had something to eat, that

he was not a homeless, and that he had the protection of a Pisces.

I know, I know. I talked a lot today, and not about the jobs. More yuca than mangoes. But I promise that I will go to the interview you made for me and do everything you say in these papers.

GENTRIFIED, RENT-STABILIZED BUILDING

Little Dominican Republic/Washington Heights
A block away from the train station
Low-performing school zip code
Neighborhood scout report: Most dangerous area to live in
Website: www.rentinnyc.org
Email address: rentinfo@rentinnyc.org
Date: October 2007

RIGHTS AND OBLIGATIONS

OF TENANTS AND LANDLORDS

UNDER THE RENT STABILIZATION LAW

Previous Legal Regulated Rent: one-third below market.

Lease Start Date: Sometime in Fall 1982
Lease End Date: Sometime in Fall 2010
Lease Dated: Renewed every two years

Guidelines

Increases for Renewal

The owner is entitled to increase the rent when the lease is over, but only within the percentage set by law. That's the benefit of being in a rent-stabilized building. It's not like the owner can raise the rent three times more. If they try to, and they might, report them.

You have the right to choose between a one-year lease or a two-year lease. The percentage for a two-year lease is higher than the one-year lease. The advantage of a two-year lease is that your rent won't go up again in one year. The disadvantage is if you move before the lease is over, you will lose your security deposit.

Appliances

Tenant agrees not to install, operate or place in the Apartment Unit any freezer, stove, cooking device, air-conditioning unit, clothes dryer, washing machine, nor any other major appliance not otherwise provided or authorized in writing by Landlord.

Succession Rights

In the event your mother or father dies or leaves to Dominican Republic, because they are one of the lucky ones who were able to buy a house and return back home, the family member who lived with them in the apartment as a primary residence for at least two years immediately prior to them leaving has the right to renew the lease.

(For family members who are senior citizens and disabled persons, you only have to prove residency for one year to inherit their apartment. We really don't like to advertise this.)

Family Member includes:

Fernando (son)
Ángela (Cara's sister)
Rafa (Cara's brother)
Family member also includes: daughter, stepson, stepdaughter, father, mother, stepfather, stepmother, grandfather, grandmother, grandson, granddaughter, father-in-law, mother-in-law, son-in-law, and daughter-in-law.

And what if you're not blood related or in-lawed?
If you can prove you have an emotional and financial
commitment and interdependence with the person who has
passed on or who has left you for another person, country, or
life, all you need to do is to provide evidence.

Evidence to prove a financial and legal connection:
Show proof that you shared a joint bank account, household
expenses such as rent or utility bills, or owned property
together. You can show a legal link by naming each other in a
will or life insurance policy and listing each other as a Health
Care Proxy or Power of Attorney. Listing each other as an
emergency contact is also helpful.

Proof of an emotional connection includes family pictures at a
birthday, holiday, religious celebration, or family events and/or
exchanging gifts/cards and sharing of responsibilities, such as
picking up children from school.

**What to avoid if you plan on succeeding someone in an
apartment:**
Do not sign a lease in the former tenant's name. Do not keep
ties with other residences or have the former tenant visit too
frequently or allow them to leave their belongings. It is also
important to document that you are paying rent. Paying with a
check or money order is best.

GENTRIFIED
RENT-STABILIZED BUILDING, INC.

BILLING INVOICE #452738

Little Dominican Republic
New York, NY 10032

To: Cara Romero

INVOICE

MONTH RENT (FEB 2009)	$888.00
OPEN BALANCE	$1,200.00
PAYMENT RECEIVED (02/05/09):	−$450.00
LATE FEE:	$40.00

Remaining Balance $1,678.00

Rent is due on the 1st of the month. Please pay rent on time to avoid late charges.

SESSION FOUR

I'm not in a good feeling today. I know we need to work, but I need to tell you what happened.

The new manager of our building came this morning to inspect the apartment. This is what they do, supposedly document repairs that have to be done. But I know the truth: it's to find reasons to throw us out.

Yes, yes. I have all my papers in order. I owe a little rent, but not much. I had to spend some money on that down payment of the surgery.

The building manager looks like the religious men that stand by the entrance of the train, with the white shirts inside their pants. He made a smile that goes up on one side and down on the other. He pretended to be innocent and this made me want to give him a pela. He walked inside with his forms and went direct to the kitchen to look at the plants I have on the fire escape. He told me if I don't take them away the fire department will give me a ticket. Is that true? You don't know? But you work for the city. This is something you should know.

The building manager looked around for everything: to the floor, to the ceiling, to the sofá, to the curtains.

Where is the smoke detector? he asked.

I told him, Every time I turn on the stove, it goes: Fire! Fire! Fire! It beeps so loud I get a migraine.

I know, don't tell me. I should put it back.

He made a little note in his papers. Like you're doing now.

What will you do with all these notes? A report? About me. You will make me look good, no?

Anyways. When he checked the radiator, I closed the curtain so he could not see the air conditioner in the window. It does not have the brackets. But tell me, you, when did an air conditioner fall out of the window and crack a person's head?

Oh, really? That happens? What a terrible thing to happen to people!

OK, OK, so then he opened the bathroom door. He saw my panties hanging to dry, and ay, Dios mío, his face was like a tomato. And, from nowhere, Lulú appeared. Yes, Lulú! She finally appeared, and she had sirenas going off in every direction.

I said, mujer, I've been looking for you! I was so worried! But she didn't care about me.

She started yelling to the building manager: I've been calling you for weeks, months, about the leak in the bathroom!

He dropped his pen and papers.

It's true, Lulú had a leak for many months, and I know because she accused *me* of throwing water on the floor, and I told her, I don't do that. Then she came to flush my toilet and turn on the water in the sink to see if it was my fault. I can't believe she didn't trust me, but OK, people are like that.

Miss, the building manager asked Lulú, in what apartment do you live?

But Lulú exploded, her mouth shoot words like a machine gun: ¡pa pa pa pa pa pa pa! With every word he step back and back and back, because Lulú is Leo with Aries rising:

fuego-fuego, with the big orange hair, she scare people. The manager pretend his phone ring and ring, lifting his finger, saying, one minute, one minute. He then disappeared down the stairs. Lulú followed him. So I followed her, grabbed her arm to stop her.

Let me go! she yelled to me.

I didn't let go. I waited for her to calm down. Then I asked her, Where have you been?

You have no idea what's happening to me, she said.

And then, I saw her face. She has not been sleeping. Bags under the eyes, no lipstick, not even earrings. I had a feeling this had to be about Adonis. What else could torment a mother like this that she would stop taking care of herself?

Her son Adonis is in trouble. But not a little trouble. Big trouble. Adonis lost his apartment. Her son, the big professional that was making four, five times what we made in the factory, lost his apartment in Brooklyn with a view of Manhattan.

Tell me, you, didn't he see those people in the news that lost their houses and are camping in the highway? What was he thinking? He bought his apartment, all of it, with a loan. Even his down payment was a loan! The banks call it a balloon—and it popped. The party is finished for Adonis.

Lulú received this bad news when she cashed the last of the unemployment checks. She always made me feel like una vieja because she was more young than me, but now she wants to be old like me so she could do this program and get the benefit checks. Her only income is what she makes working in the bodega. She can't help her son. Lulú is very humiliated about Adonis. This is why she avoid me. She was afraid to tell me. But I don't judge. To be a mother is to suffer.

You try and try with the children and they step on shit anyway. It's too bad because in truth our children have it more easy than us.

Lulú never took the side of his son's wife, Patricia. She mopped the floor with Patricia's name because, according to Lulú, Patricia never contributes to the rent. She only pays the phone and the electricity, and she makes Adonis do all the laundry for the house. Lulú hates Patricia for that.

She always says, Look at my poor son, working like an animal so that woman can spend her weekends fixing her hair in the salón. But Patricia's not a pendeja. Women know that if we don't put in all that work, men like Adonis, that love shiny things, would have eyes on someone else, and fast. But Lulú has no sympathy for Patricia, who works in an office for a lawyer. I am sure, too, that she does most of the work with the babies.

Ángela and I never agree, but when we talk about Patricia and Adonis, we agree on this: Patricia was intelligent to put half of her check in a separate bank account. And thank God Adonis refused to marry her with papers. The relief that woman must feel now—legally free from Adonis, his debt, and his bad credit. If she had not saved her own money, Patricia and her babies would be left with nothing.

Women know even the things we don't see. Yes or no?

¡Ay! But what I was trying to tell you is that I am worried about the changes the building is trying to make. Every time the management makes improvements they make more rules. Look at what happened to my neighbor Tita that lived in the building for more long than me. She did not take the washing machine out of the apartment—and the new lease says No Washing Machine. The management sent a letter to Tita many months ago to say that if she didn't take out the machine in ten days she and her daughter Cecilia must leave the apartment because she violated the lease! Violated. Tita is cabeza dura so she didn't take out the machine because she uses the washing machine almost every day. Her daughter Cecilia makes, all the time, a big mess. All of us thought the management, maybe this once, was going to break the rules for Tita, because she lived in the apartment for many decades, and her daughter has a disability. But they have no feelings.

Yes, yes, Tita went to the court. Lulú made Patricia to help Tita. But this is another opportunity for the management to rent an apartment for three times the price we pay. She had a big apartment with two bedrooms. And because Tita did not want to leave the building and be far away from us, she moved downstairs to the one-bedroom with the windows looking to the brick wall. And the rent is now $450 more than what she paid.

Me? Oh, don't worry. I'm OK. Yes, I pay rent every month. Sometimes I owe a little. But not too much. If we pay the rent, and don't break the rules of the lease, Patricia told me that the management can't throw us out. They would have to give us many money to leave. I can pay everything when I find a job. You will help me find a job, yes?

Ay, I get nervous because very easily, after working so hard, you can be with nothing. Pobrecita Tita. One day, she is ready to retire to have an easy life, and the next day, her life is an infierno. The management have many properties in all of New York. They are so rich, why do this to Tita? We all had washing machines for many years but that was no problem because nobody wanted to live in Washington Heights, only us. But now everybody wants to live in Washington Heights because it's not expensive like downtown. And now the area has the white people bar, and the white people gourmet bodega, and the $15 white people personal pizza, not even for a family. Fifteen dollars for one person!

Tita thought she could live with the Social Security and the disability. With the low rent, it was enough. But listen to me, there is never rest for the poor. Now pobrecita Tita can't pay for her new apartment, so she can't retire—she had to take a job. A terrible job. She saw a paper in the train that said: *$10 an hour! No experience necessary!* Yes, that's right, the one you see all the time written by hand on a paper bag. For two days a week, she works, taking care of a vieja. They pay her in cash so she can still get her benefits. But the lady she works for makes Tita sleep on the floor next to her bed. She wants to see Tita all the time.

Yes, it's true. Incredible.

On the floor! On a yoga mat!

The lady told her that the mat is very comfortable. That in many parts of the world, people sleep on the floor and how good sleeping on the floor will be for Tita's back. Can you believe it? Even when la vieja has another room with a good bed. She doesn't care that Tita is old like her. It's true she looks good for her age. But to make a human being sleep on the floor? No. And what is Tita going to do? She needs the money.

Of course, if I am desperate I would do like Tita. But I hope at this stage of my life, I am never so desperate.

Tita is a saint. She works for this lady in the night and

does not complain because she prefers to give her daughter the medicine that makes her sleep for ten hours and go to work. That way Cecilia doesn't see that Tita is gone.

So this week, and until Tita doesn't have to do this terrible job, all of us in the building take turns with Cecilia. Tita's apartment is downstairs. Her apartment shares a wall with Lulú. This is good because we use the walkie-talkie. If Cecilia wakes up we can run to see if she is OK. Cecilia is not developed in the brain, so she's like a baby and can't walk—but she's forty years old. Most nights Tita says she is calm, but sometimes she wakes up scared, so we listen just in case. She usually gives no problem, but a few days ago when it was my turn, Cecilia woke up screaming, full of terror. And ay, Dios mío, when I arrived, Cecilia was screaming so loud, one hand covering the ear, one arm waving up and down and up and down, the hand hitting the mattress. The neighbors came of their apartments. The feathers from inside the pillows were everywhere. The plant, the soil was on the floor. Everything around was broken.

My neighbor Glendaliz said, I'm calling the ambulance.

Let's call the police, a tall flaco said. Because you know that's what our new neighbors do now. Any little noise and they call the policía.

No, wait, I said. Nothing good comes from calling the police. They can report Tita and social services can take Cecilia.

In America the authorities do many things that don't make sense to me.

I've known Cecilia almost all of her life, so I was not afraid of her. The others were afraid because Cecilia does this thing with her eyes where she looks up and around, and her scream—it's not a scream, it's like *Eeeeeeeeeee!*—like an ice pick stabbing in the ears. I sat next to her and, really fast, I grabbed her with all the strength in my body. I trapped her arms inside mine and I held her fuerte, fuerte and I did a sound like *Huuuuuuuummmmmmmmmmmm.* She could feel the hum in my body against her body. You know how the engine feels under the legs when you sit all the way in the back of the bus. *Huummmmmmmmmm.*

And she stopped moving back and forth. She got calm. When you have children—oh, that's right, you don't want children. Well, I knew what to do because I did it when Fernando was a baby. It works like magic. Cecilia went to sleep.

After, I told everybody to leave—because some people were looking at Cecilia like she was a show. I was alone in the apartment. It was so small. Dique a one-bedroom, but really it was two rooms. Tita took the bedroom and has Cecilia sleeping in the living room. It's one of those salas where one wall has the kitchen and the other wall has the sofa bed. I tell you, very small. So small that if you sit on the sofa bed, you can touch the stove. That's where Cecilia sleeps. Why do they make apartments like this? I don't understand why anybody would not want a wall to separate the kitchen grease from the furniture. It's obviously an apartment for someone that does not cook, that does not prepare food; they put two or three things together and say dinner is ready. They only boil water for the tea or an egg.

The window looks to a brick wall, so I can imagine it's very dark during the day. How can people live without light? Qué tristeza.

It's like living in a closet. Pobrecita Tita lives in a closet.

I could have gone back to my apartment and sleep, but

I stayed with Cecilia because I was awake. So I cleaned. Nobody wants to come home to a mess. I didn't want Tita to see all the broken glass and feathers. I tried to wash away the smell of Band-Aid and humidity that gives me the náusea, because like you know I'm very sensitive to smell. But Tita can't help it. All those years working in the hospital, all the bottles of sanitizer and antiseptic she brought home.

So I opened the windows to refresh the air and emptied out the fridge. Wiped clean the crusted bottle tops. Cleaned all the shelves, scraped the frost off the freezer walls. She had only been in the apartment a few weeks, but already the freezer had frost. I scrubbed the oxidación off the sink. I boiled canela and naranja peel so the apartment smelled like un postre. And between us, after I was done, it was a different apartment. No offense to Tita. I mopped the floors two times.

Yes, I don't mind to clean. To do it every day for money, I don't know. I can think about that. We can talk about the possibilities.

But what I was saying is that I waited for Tita to arrive sitting on a hard chair. It was so uncomfortable, a torture really, looking to the brick wall outside the window. The only light was a horrible fluorescent bulb in the ceiling.

What kind of life is this? She lives in el closet and the rent more than what she used to pay. She works every minute she's not taking care of her daughter.

At least in my apartment I have a view from the living room window. On a clear day, I swear to you, I can see the George Washington Bridge. To have a view in Manhattan is not nothing. Even when I can't go anywhere, because to leave the apartment is to lose money, I look to the big things of New York—it's very beautiful. All these buildings, trees. The way the sky changes color. The way the trees have different seasons. I can't imagine what it's like to live inside, encerrá, in the winter especially, with nowhere to go, looking to a brick wall, with no space to move. It hurts me. I feel sad for Tita, but also for me because her story makes me think one can't predict what will happen in life.

Let me tell you about one time, a long time ago, when I was in Hato Mayor and there was a hurricane. It hit my mother's house. I was still married to Ricardo. Visiting my parents. Fernando had one year. Only a few hours before, it was a beautiful day. Nobody knew the storm was coming. The government didn't tell us. The radio didn't warn us. Y, *prá!* The water turned all the streets into a river. Two of my cousins drowned that day.

The government knew that the storm was strong, but they didn't want any pánico, so they didn't sound the alarm. The sky got green and then black in five minutes. We moved the furniture into one room, closed the doors. We put tape on the windows. We heard the trees crash, the gritos of the neighbors. Then the water was all around us. I saw a car flying. It's true. The hurricane gave us a pela.

And then it stopped. I thought, *OK, OK, now we can go back to normal.*

Pfft! How could we go back to normal?

We could not trust the beautiful sky. We could not trust the government to be honest with us. We lost many people. Many properties were destroyed. Eight children died inside a school. It collapsed on them. Can you believe it?

So of course, we were all paranoicos. We thought maybe the government is trying to kill us. Every time, I tell you, every time we saw a dark cloud, our bodies got tense. Everyone knows that hurricanes are like jealous lovers. One follows the other.

One day, my uncle Rufino was fishing and he saw the water of the sea getting bigger and bigger. He went home and told his wife, Clarissa. Then Clarissa said she had a dream about another hurricane coming—and we all know Clarissa's dreams are true, like a contract. And then, when her neighbor heard about the dream of the storm, she told her cousin in New York. And the cousin in New York then told her sister, that called her mother in Santo Domingo. Phones were ringing from New York to Hato Mayor to Copellito and then to La Capital. And then we were convinced that this storm was going to be more strong than the last one. Because not only Clarissa was dreaming the storm, but everyone was waking up with the thoughts of the rain and the flying trees.

So even if the sun was shining, and the radio played bachata and the DJ in the radio was talking vaina, we were sure another hurricane was coming. So we packed our photos and important papers inside the big plastic garbage bags. We prepared our windows. We closed all our doors. We drove up to the highest hill and waited for it.

The santeras lit their candles and sacrificed some animals, and the rest of us prayed to La Virgen de Altagracia, because even if she usually forgets about us, it's better to have faith in something than nothing. We waited inside a big house made of cement. An abandoned palace owned by a baseball player that gambled and lost all his money. Long time abandoned, without electricity or water, but it was high on the hill, so it was safe from flooding.

I was sure we were going to die.

And you know what I thought? *Does it really matter if I die?*

I was married.

I had a child.

I had lived enough.

And you know what? The storm never came! So, you see, that's the thing when you grow up in a place like Hato Mayor. You can plan all you want, but nature will always show you who's el jefe.

Learn this from me. So much can happen in the life. Things you did not imagine. When I was a girl, I never imagined I was going to be sitting here with you. In New York. With a husband that almost killed me, and a son that will not return home.

So, like I was saying, we can't always plan what is going to happen. But who knows, maybe praying together to La Virgen made the hurricane disappear. Maybe if we work together, we can find a solution to my problem.

Yes, of course. I promise, next week I will take the test you ask of me. If we don't get on the bike and peddle, for sure we get nowhere.

CAREER SKILLS MATCHER

Your source for career exploration, training, and jobs
Find the best job for your personality and interests
Sponsored by the Senior Workforce Program

The jobs on this report may be good matches for your workstyle, based on how you rated your skills, interests, and personality.

Skills you rated highest:

- Work with disabled persons
- Teach social skills to children
- Research new medicine
- Install a hardwood floor
- Persuade others to one's point of view
- Write a script for a television show
- Counsel a person with depression
- Plan educational games for preschool children
- Plan activities for the elderly
- Give a speech in front of many people

Personality traits you rated highest:

- Shy
- Inquisitive
- Reserved
- Agreeable
- Creative
- Self-disciplined
- Outgoing
- Charitable

- Organized
- Humble

Your WORKSTYLE results:

Cara Romero, you are a **HUMANITARIAN**! You want to make the world a better place.

Cara Romero, you are a **CARETAKER**! You are of service to others.

Cara Romero, you are an **INNOVATOR**! You can solve complex, rational problems.

Cara Romero, you are a **PRAGMATIST**! You are accurate and efficient.

Cara Romero, you are an **OBSERVER**! You notice details and make connections.

The best career choice for Cara Romero is **HELPING.** You want to dedicate your work life to serving, caring for, and inspiring others, motivated by an aspiration to make the world a better place. You are highly attuned to the needs of the people around you and gain satisfaction from attending to those needs. Other strengths include: **BUILDING, THINKING, CREATING, PERSUADING, ORGANIZING.**

Our top careers for Cara Romero:

(You must meet the education and experience requirements before applying.)

- Certified Occupational Therapy Assistant to help patients develop, recover, improve, as well as maintain the skills needed for daily living and working.
- Career or Technical Teacher in auto repair, cosmetology, and culinary arts.

- Emergency Management Director for national disasters and other emergencies.

Cara Romero, explore your next career by calling us at The Job You Want & Co.

THE JOB YOU WANT & CO.

Company: Seize Life Assisted Living

POSITION DESCRIPTION

We are looking for experienced and energetic Housekeepers to help create a clean, warm, and comfortable environment for our Residents. The Housekeeper will clean Resident apartments, restrooms, common areas, as well as the office and surrounding areas according to housekeeping standards and procedures.

Qualifications: A pleasant and courteous demeanor when dealing with peers, supervisors, guests, residents, and management. Must be very thorough with cleaning practices. Experience providing cleaning services in the restaurant, healthcare, hospital, hotel, hospitality, or similar industry is required. Experience working with a senior population is preferred. Ability to work in a fast-paced environment while dealing with a demanding customer. Must be able to communicate in English, including keeping inventory and filling out supply order forms.

Location: El Barrio, New York
Department: Housekeeping
Starting salary: $10.00 an hour
Position type: Full-time shift: 8:00 a.m.–4:00 p.m. (M–F)

PREPARING FOR THE INTERVIEW:

HOUSEKEEPING

Your future employer will be interested in knowing about your work experience. It is best to be specific and give concrete examples about why you enjoy working as a housekeeper. Remember to smile and show your enthusiasm for housekeeping. When answering the interview questions, think about what tasks you would be happiest doing the most. Arrive to the interview prepared with answers.

Examples of interview questions and answers

Interviews require practice. Find a volunteer who will ask you the practice interview questions so you are prepared to answer them. Below is an example of how to answer. Use it as inspiration.

Common interview questions

What housekeeping tasks do you enjoy the most?
What housekeeping tasks do you enjoy the least?
What is the most rewarding part of housekeeping?
What skills do you have that make you right for this job?
What housekeeping skills could you improve on?

What do you enjoy most about housekeeping?
Example answer: I enjoy many aspects of housekeeping. I feel immense satisfaction when I have the opportunity to organize a messy room. This includes making the bed and folding the sheets. It is very relaxing to fold sheets. I find it to be quite therapeutic. I want people to return to their rooms and see the difference I have made in their lives!

SESSION FIVE

Before you say something, you have to try my arepitas de yuca. I fried them for you this morning. Guayé la yuca and then I mixed it with one egg and some salt and anís. So simple. But not many people make it like me. See how it's crispy outside and the inside is juicy? You like them?

No, I didn't go to the interview last week. Did they call you to tell you that? Interesting.

It was in El Barrio! First, El Barrio is too far. I saw the map. To get to 100th Street and First Avenue, it's two trains, one bus, and many, many blocks to walk. I know we agreed that I will interview for jobs less than five miles away. But it's not the miles, it's the time. From here to there it's more than one hour! It's no good for me. Too many people depend on me.

Who? The children of Ángela and Hernán that I take to their activities after they get out of the school.

Yes, I know this is only temporary until they leave. But now they depend on me.

And there is La Vieja Caridad, that leaves me messages in my machine, exactly at 4:45 p.m. every day.

Cara, you home?

I'll translate for you: Cara, did you cook for me today?

Nobody eats at five! But it's no big thing to prepare dinner for her.

Yes, yes, come down, I tell her. I never say no to La Vieja Caridad. If I make it to ninety years, maybe a vecina will do the same for me.

Anyways, she eats like una pajarita. I make the grilled fish, very plain, only a little salt and limon, the arroz jasmine only, because if not the cheap arroz make everybody inflate like a whale. I cook the vegetables so they melt in the mouth. She can't chew. And every night she has to drink a cold beer. One entire bottle. She says it's her secret to a long life.

When La Vieja Caridad eats she likes to talk, so we talk. Yesterday was the anniversary of her friend's death that had lived with her for many decades. She said to me, I should've not lost so much time being afraid of her dying.

But that's normal, I told her. It's difficult to lose your friend. Everybody gets afraid.

We should be more like the animals, she said. The animals don't think of the future or the past; they pay attention to what is happening in the present. It is enough to sit with a person. To brush the hair. To massage the feet. To bring them what they need. We can't fight what we can't control. She said she missed her friend's last breath because she was busy with the hope. She should have been breathing with her.

I worry about La Vieja Caridad because I can smell the cancer on her, just like with Glendaliz, but she won't check the blood. But she is right; I can't make her check. Learn this from me: If you try to fix something that somebody do not want to fix they will hate you for it. To offer help is OK. To push, no.

So you see, if I go to work in El Barrio, I can't make dinner for her. And that's no good for the present. Ha!

Why you can't help me find a job close to my apartment, like in the hospital? That way I can walk to work. Hernán told me there was an opportunity to work in the hospital. Not in his kitchen; in another kitchen in another building.

You heard about that job? No? He doesn't even know if they advertise because, I told you, for everything around here you need a key. Can you find out for me? Because I need your help for this.

Maybe you know Hernán. No? Everybody knows Hernán. He's bald like an egg, with hair that grows out his ears. Not ugly. Just not the kind of man that you would be *wow*, right away.

In the hospital, Hernán is loved. I don't recommend hospital food to nobody. I don't know how people feel better drinking that hot and dirty water they call soup. Everybody knows for the sopa to be good you have to boil the bones. The nutrients are in the bones. You need the salt to activate it. A lot of garlic and onion. Some carrots or auyama and celery for sure. And when it's hot-hot and it has been boiling for an hour, you strain it. And if you want to go crazy put a little vinegar to make it alive, but also vinegar cures everything. It makes a difference when you cut the vegetables and think, *This sopa is going to make you feel better.* Sometimes I ask myself, with all the schools people go to, all the money in this country, why people don't know how to make a good sopa. It's sad to heat a soup from a can or mix powder into hot water.

Learn this from me: Eating food from the streets will kill you. It's dead food.

And this is why Hernán is especial—in the good way. Hernán's cooking is better than any restaurant. Even when the hospital says no to all his ideas, because dique the budget, he knows how to resolver. He saves the scraps from the vegetables and puts them in the caldo. Nothing is wasted in his kitchen. He makes the hospital food good because he cares.

And you know why Hernán is such a good cook? Because I invent in the kitchen and I teach him everything I know. That's right!

Write that down: Cara Romero likes to invent.

I am not surprised that that test said I am an Innovator. I've been thinking about that test. How it says I'm good at helping and I'm good to organize. And I think that's true about me.

An example? Hmm. I have many examples of when I organized in the factory. I will tell you this one. Every day, we had to make a certain number of lamparita pieces. Then one day, they increased our numbers. El jefe had pressure to meet the orders. He didn't want us to talk, because if we talked, or listened to the radio, we were more slow. I was always good with my numbers but Lulú, no.

This is the thing, when Lulú was working in the sewing factory downtown, the *télele-télele* of sewing machines ruined Lulu's wrists; that vibration is a killer. That's why I got her a job in our factory. And for a time she was doing better, but again she was feeling the pain. In her arms, her neck, her back, from sitting many hours. I felt the pain too, but I'm accustomed to it. Lulú likes to complain.

Me, I'm a fast worker. El jefe would say, Cara give me 3000 pieces, I made 5000. That's why they called me La Maquineta. I was proud of my numbers too. But if I went too fast, Lulú, Doña Lilina, and Doña Altagracia looked too slow.

Hurry up, el jefe told las doñas, that have almost seventy years and had the arthritis in the knees and the hips. He said this to Lulu too, when she dropped the merchandise to the floor because she couldn't feel her fingers.

Go to the doctor, I always told Lulú. And one time, she

did. But the doctor said she should take a vacation to rest her hands and arms. He said to apply for worker's comp. Ha! The factory wanted to lay off people. Most of the people on probation never became permanent. Even before the crisis, we heard of factorías going to other countries. And we liked our job. Some of the jefes were good to us. Well, they paid us very punctual every week. And overtime.

The doctor said that if Lulú couldn't take a vacation, she should take short breaks through the day. The doctor said we should all take breaks, even for one minute: a break every thirty minutes, to stretch the legs and the hands. Very important. If not, we'll have the pain. Sitting all day is more bad for the health than smoking a cigarette. But we're not permitted to stop working so we can stretch our legs. And no note from the doctor was going to convince el jefe. Look, when they started laying off people, we never stopped, even to use the bathroom.

Now you will see why I'm a good organizer. I made a secret meeting during lunch. I told the young ones what the doctor said. And if the jefes won't give us the breaks, we have to steal the breaks. If we work together, we can do the job, and not destroy our bodies. Also, because some people are slower, when we finish our quotas, we should help the others. It worked. We took turns to take small, one-minute breaks and still made the numbers without el jefe noticing. We were like a family and took care of each other. The new girls didn't understand this in the beginning, but when they paid attention to me, they became one of us.

Your little test is correct. I am an Organizer.

But I'm also a Pragmatist, and I understand that, even in organizing, not everybody cooperates and every secret plan has to remain secret until people can prove you can trust them. I am like the ducks that sleep with one eye open.

For example, María I didn't trust. She wasn't invited to the meetings. She had a mouth like a mop: picking up the dirt from all the corners. When el jefe David invited her to his office to *talk* about her *hours,* he squeezed the dirt out of her.

María was a flaca with little baby hands and hair that passed her butt, so heavy, her head leaned back from the weight. We knew she chupa chupa the boss's lollipop for overtime hours. But I don't judge. Women have to do what they have to do to survive. So we were good to María, and laughed with her at lunch—until she told el jefe that I was taking home the toilet paper.

OK, don't look at me this way. I only took it because the extra step to go to the bodega after a long day of work, especially when it was snowing, was too much for me. María, green like a baby guineo, knows nothing about life.

One day, when I offered María a pastelito and she said no thank you, I knew I had to be careful. No one says no to my pastelitos. My neighbor Ana gave me all her secrets before she moved to Boston. When I tell you they're good, I mean good. Even if you're not hungry, you take it and save it for later. One day I will bring you one, so you understand.

So I didn't take the toilet paper that day, just in case. When el jefe went to look in my things, my bag was clean. I knew it!

Anyways, why do they care? It's toilet paper!

But that's not the point. The point is that I have many talents. More than appears in your test, if you can believe it. Like my nose, for example. Remember how I told you I can smell the cancer?

Write that down: Cara Romero can smell the sickness.

And the reason I know this is because, one time, my brother Rafa came to stay with me after his wife, Miguelina, threw him out. When Rafa drinks, he likes to hit, like my ex-husband, Ricardo. But Miguelina is slow to learn. The first time he hit her she fell and broke her forehead on the table and almost lost an eye. But did she leave him? No. She kept ironing the shirts and cooking the dinner, even when he was staying with some fulana that sold numbers. He liked to bet on the numbers, so he had a good excuse to go over there.

Every woman has a limit, and Rafa did something to Miguelina that she couldn't forgive. What does this have to do with my nose? Wait, wait, I'll get there. You're very impatient.

One day, Miguelina was coming home late from Bronx Community College. It's been forever that Miguelina's been trying to get a nursing degree. She got the idea to go to school from Ángela. It's like saving money. A little bit of sacrifice. A little bit of patience. Every semester, she started those night classes, going far, far up there to the Bronx to study after working as a receptionist in the clinic. And some semesters she got those credits because, like Ángela, she was determined to finish. But I told her by the time she finished, she'd be ready to retire.

You see, Ángela finished her degree to be an accountant because she's married to Hernán. If you're lucky you find a man that you don't fall in the hole with. Miguelina was married to my brother, a ship with many holes.

But anyways, there was that night where the bus was not in service. It was a Thursday. By Thursday even I'm exhausted.

Even without night school, I feel like anything can break me.
So, with good reason, Miguelina took a taxi home. But Rafa's
an ignorant. He's my brother, but I'm sure he was dropped
by my mother to the floor more than one time when he was
a baby. That night she took a taxi and realized she didn't have
any money. She was sure she had put it inside the small pocket
of her purse, but it was not there. When she arrived to the
apartment, she told Rafa in the intercom to come down to
pay for it.

You know what he did? He yelled, Woman, why are you
bothering me? I'm sleeping! I have to work tomorrow! He
had too much to drink to think correct. One or two drinks,
fine. But when a person has too much, they only think about
themselves—so selfish!

Poor Miguelina. Thank God they live down the street
from me. She buzzed me and I felt so bad for her. The humiliation! Of course, I went down and paid for the taxi, and we
never talked about it again.

When Miguelina found out that this fulana was driving
around in a new car that Rafa was paying for every month,
something broke in her. For more than a year, Rafa paid
$229 a month for that woman's car. And then, with another
face, he called Miguelina a princess for taking a taxi after
working all day and going to school in the night. *Pfft!*

I knew the day would come when she changed the locks.
Left his clothes in a bag outside the door. That's how it happens. Especially with quiet women like Miguelina.

So what was I supposed to do? Rafa's my brother. I couldn't
let him sleep in the streets. Ángela, who wore the T-shirt of YO
SOY FEMINISTA, was on Miguelina's side. Lulú told me it was a
big mistake to accept Rafa in my apartment. She said, This is

why men don't change. When the women try to teach a man a lesson, here come the mothers and the sisters to save them.

But Lulú, what if it was your son, Adonis?

A few days of sleeping in the streets would not kill him, she said. Ha! This she said back then because she couldn't imagine the trouble Adonis is in now.

Listen, I know Rafa is no good. I know Lulú is correct. The only way he will change is if he sleeps in the streets. But, I'm sorry, I'm not so strong to see him live like he doesn't have family. I can't do it.

You can stay for two weeks, I said. Not one day more.

He stayed three months.

The reason I say to you this story is because from the first day he stayed with me I could smell the sweet smell of nail polish in the salón. I mopped the floors with Pine Sol, but the smell parked itself in my sala.

I asked Lulú, Ángela, and Tita to come over, to see if they could smell it.

Rafa was sleeping on the sofa still wearing his mechanic's uniform. They couldn't smell anything. Ángela thought it was my menopausia.

She said, Some women lose their smell, but you have the opposite.

I said, Maybe it's Rafa. Does he smell strange to you?

Tell him to take a shower, they laughed. They insisted it was all in my head. But the day Rafa moved out of my apartment, the smell disappeared. When he came for un café, the smell returned.

I told him to go to the doctor to get a chequeo. I knew he was sick before he complained his eyes were bad. Not all the time, just some of the time. Even when he ate like a pig he got flaco like a spaghetti. He was always tired, sweating when it was cold.

Then the doctor told him: he had the diabetes. The nail polish smell was the diabetes.

I didn't make the connection immediately. I had to smell a few people. Sometimes the smell was very specific. My nose is better than those strips from the doctor. The more sugar in the blood, the more strong the smell.

Tell someone the drinking will kill them, and they go drink anyways. Sometimes Rafa's eyes were so bad that when he was driving he only knew he had to stop because he hit something. And his foot turned different colors and the doctor told him, if he continued, he would have to cut off his toes. You think he cared?

Cut them. I rather have no legs than stop living my life, he said.

And when Miguelina refused to accept him back, la fulana who got his $229 a month for the car *rented* him a room in her apartment.

Women are so desperate! And what company is Rafa? He's a man that says nothing, and with the sugar in his blood, he can't get up his lollipop. I'm serious! That's what Miguelina says.

OK, OK, yes, back to the test. Yes, it's very good! It helped me a lot. This test has me thinking that it's true: I am a good Caretaker, I am a good Organizer, I am a Pragmatist, I am an Observer, I am good for helping old people. I never thought that I was good for managing emergency disasters. But maybe yes!

Remember the building manager that came to inspect our apartments? Well, this was a good thing for Lulú. Most of the time we pay somebody we know to fix things. But now we don't have the money. The building only comes to check what we do wrong, not to fix the things. But we know we have rights. This we learned when we went to La Escuelita. La Profesora said, not even the police can do what they want. If they stop us, we have rights not to talk. If they come to our apartment, we have rights not to open the door.

The point is, like I told you before, Lulú had complained to management more than once and they did not answer her call. So you can imagine—drip and drip and drip. One pot full of water a day. And the water balloon on her ceiling went from the size of a limoncillo, to an orange, to a big lechosa.

When the other people that pay three times what we pay for the rent call the super, immediately the super fixes it. They see a mouse, the super tapa the holes. They have a leak in their sink, the super runs to make the leak stop. Before these other people moved in, the super always had time for us. Well, the old super had time for us. This new super is a friend of nobody.

I think the management pays him a bonus every time one of us moves out.

I tell you, we try to be patient, me more than Lulú. But we have only limited patience. Imagine how scared was Lulú when a piece of the ceiling fell on her head. She made a grito so loud, I heard it from my apartment. I called her to make sure she was OK, Then I came down with the camera. There she was, under a chorro de agua because the water balloon on the ceiling popped. *Prá!* What a mess. Water everywhere. Dirty water. With it came down part of the ceiling. All the wood was rotten. It was an emergency. Thank God I was there. I told her to lay down on the ground so I could take a good photo to show that the ceiling could have assassinated her.

I took many photos. I told Lulú, Stay on the floor and wait for me to come back with the super, so he can see with his own eyes. It worked. The super fixed the problem the same day.

After, the building manager came to check the job. He asked Lulú to sign papers, but I said, No. Don't sign papers without your lawyer. Lulú made a strange face, but I know when you say lawyer, people are more careful.

So, you see, like this paper says, I could also be a good Emergency Management Director for national disasters and emergencies. Ha!

Is that a job I can do from my apartment?

INTERVIEW PREPARATION

When you arrive, make eye contact.

If they extend their hand, shake it.

They will tell you when and where to sit.

Remember, they interview many people in one day.

They will be taking notes that can help them capture why you're right for the job.

Make the time you have in the room count.

Answer the questions.

Do not go on tangents.

Interviewers will value your willingness to look them in the eye. If you have a difficult time looking them in the eye, look at their foreheads.

Good interviewers should put you at ease. They want to find the perfect person for the job. They will focus on why you're right for the job, not on why you're wrong.

Make sure to nod your head and smile occasionally to signal that you are listening.

Remember, you are protected from employment discrimination based on race, color, religion, sex (including pregnancy, sexual orientation, or gender identity), national origin, age (40 or older), disability, and genetic information (including family medical history).

Interviewers should not ask you questions such as: Do you go to church? How old are you? Are you married? Do you have children? Where are you from?

If they do, please feel free to report them to your case worker.

Job Position: Nanny
Candidate Name: Cara Romero
Position Description: Lovely family in Brooklyn seeks an energetic, loving, and proactive live-in nanny to provide care for their three young children. This position primarily consists of a Monday-to-Friday workweek, roughly 12 hours per day, with a midday lunch break. Responsibilities include: following a strict feeding and sleeping schedule, maintaining hygiene, meal preparation, children's laundry, playtime, organization of materials and children's items. The family will provide private accommodations inclusive of a private bedroom and bathroom.

PROSPECTIVE
EMPLOYEE QUESTIONNAIRE

Please write your answers to the questions below:

1. What attracted you to this interview opportunity? *I want werk. Thenk you.*

2. What are your long-term career goals? *I like werk. Thenk you.*

3. What makes you a good candidate for the position? *I like babys. They love me.*

4. What is your experience enforcing schedules, following recipes, etc.? *Yes, is OK. I can do.*

5. This job requires being active all day. Do you anticipate this being a problem? *No, I never sit.*

6. The job requires you to get a background check, is that OK with you? *Yes. No problem.*

7. If offered the position, when are you available to begin work? *I can werk. I want to werk. Thenk you.*

8. Do you drive? *No problem. I can lern. Thenk you.*

EVALUATION BY EMPLOYER:

Recommend to hire: Yes ☐ | No ☑ | Decision not yet made ☐
Not a match: ☑

SESSION SIX

Before you say something, I have to tell you: Alicia the Psychic wrote to me the day before I went to that interview. She said Mercury is in retrograde. You don't know what that is? Every few months for three to four weeks communication is bad. So, for example, you can't sign contracts. I told Ángela this, but she put down the deposit to secure the house in Long Island. In some place called Shirley? You know this Shirley place?

Yes, where the plane crashed in the nineties. Ángela wants to live near the beach. She shows me many photos. I don't make opinions, but why does she want to go so far away where there are no people? She will be aburrida. I am sure.

Anyways, Alicia the Psychic said I should not start something new, like a job. Yes, in her letter she said *job*. One must be very careful right now. It's not the time to make something happen. It is the time to stop and reflect.

Alicia the Psychic also said someone, dique an old lover, will turn up the fire again. But she advised I must be careful because it's a bad time for everything. Ha! An old lover? Looking for me?

The last man that came to me in that way was José. It happened many times. I mean many, many times for many years. But it was not a serious thing.

You see, José owned the Everything Store on Broadway. It literally had one of everything. And he kept the store full. And for things like a drill or a hammer he would let us borrow it if we promised to bring it back in the same condition. It's incredible he stayed in business for so long because he didn't care about making money. One day I needed to copy a key. He was busy, so instead of making me wait, he promised delivery to my apartment after he closed the store.

When he came, I invited him for un café. He must've liked how I made it because he came many times after that. I didn't think much of his visits. He had a good woman in the house. We all liked the wife, La Cubana. Later we found out she wasn't Cuban—she was from Venezuela. She was the cashier and put labels on everything so we could know the price easy. Her *qualities*, like José would call them, were good for the store. But in his house, this *quality* for organization drove José crazy. She controlled what he could eat, what he could drink, where he couldn't sit, where he couldn't put his feet.

I'm accustomed to men sitting in my kitchen and talking. José visits. Hernán visits. My brother, Rafa, visits. They visit to escape from the world, you know?

But I wasn't born yesterday. When a man complains about his wife to a woman that lives alone, you either bite, or you don't bite. I needed a distraction from thinking of Fernando. So when José came to me, I told him to sit on the sofa in the sala and to put his feet on the coffee table—with his shoes on. Ha! I served him un café, sweet like he liked it. And when he wanted to smoke a cigarillo inside, I put an ashtray on the coffee table and said: Go ahead. You need a match?

He lit a cigarette, and forget it.

Do you have whiskey? he asked.

I never have liquor in the apartment because I don't like to give it to Rafa, who always drinks until the bottle is finished.

The next time, I was ready for José. I bought a bottle of whiskey. When I poured the whiskey over some ice, the way he looked to me, ay, papá! We became like satin.

With each visit—more satin.

I look good for my age, but still, it's not every day a man appears in your door like that. José was not ugly—tall, with big shoulders and a strong nose. Are you following me? You say yes with your head like you understand, but I think you're too young to really understand. When you become my age it's not enough to eat a lot of fish and aguacate and gallons and gallons of water to keep it juicy and tight down there.

Ay, I've embarrassed you! Perdón.

It's just that I can never tell Lulú about José. If she finds out she will curse me. She wouldn't do it on purpose; a curse is something people do without conscious.

I know, I know, we have serious work to do. But let me tell you that every time José rang the doorbell—I answered. I was ready. I mean ready. I shaved my legs. I cut my hair down there. I put on fresh panties—the lacy kind. I turned off all the lights and received him smiling in the shadow.

Same like him, I needed a place to run away without rules.

I massaged his shoulders. Waited until he got comfortable. When he gave me the look, you know the look. I put the radio with the music loud and then I climbed him like a horse, with my back against his chest. We didn't look at each other. Our minds free. José grabbed me—not too hard, but with strength, you know. Ay, it felt good. He never took all the clothes off. I liked that. It made everything feel less wrong. And I pressed his hands on all my buttons, here and here and here, while he put it in me so good. ¡Ay!

He, many times, said to me, You're like a dream.

Men live on the clouds.

When he left, I put on the pajamas and put my hair in a tubi. Washed off the makeup so my face could breathe. Turned off the music and put the telenovela on. What a relief to have the apartment for myself.

Nobody needed to know what happened between us. It felt good to keep it private. Like praying. You don't have to announce that you pray. I don't need no one to make me feel bad about it. José was the antídoto to some of the most poisonous years of my life. He filled the emptiness of my apartment.

Listen to me, it's good to be reminded we are alive. For this, Hernán is good.

No, don't look at me like that. We are family. But he is still a man and he would be dead if he didn't react to me.

One time Julio poured milk on my shirt. What a disaster. It went down my blusa and pants. I had to take everything off. That day I was watching the children in the apartment of Ángela. So I went to her closet, but that flaca has nothing that fits me. So I looked in Hernán's closet. OK, I admit I like the smell of sweat and colonia. And then I heard my name in that fatherly voice of Hernán.

Cara?

He was standing in the entrance of the bedroom. I had left the door open to hear the children.

¡Mira coño! My towel fell to the floor. Thank God my back was to him. I covered my tetas with my hand and picked up the towel. It was like I was caught stealing. What was I going to do? I was only wearing panties. Then I saw him looking at me on the mirror in the wall on the other side of the room.

Standing there like a statue. I was like a statue too. Then I dropped the towel again. And there it was. Impossible not to see—Hernán was hard like un pilón.

No wonder Ángela was so jealous with Hernán. He is a bombón. I mean not guapo-handsome like for the movies, more gentle and sexy, like San Francis. You know, the saint that loves the animals?

So yes, this too, I have no one to talk about.

Ay, Dios, what happens to me in your office. I talk and talk.

Yes, I'll drink some water.

Maybe it's because the lights here are so bright, the walls look like a face without makeup. Why you don't wear makeup? You're young. This is the time to find someone. You don't *like* makeup? You only need a little bit. I'm sure you see all the scrunchy around my eyes, on all my face. You put on the cream, no? Every day, you have to wear the cream and a big hat so the sun doesn't get you. I didn't know this when I was your age. Look at my forehead—the lines are making me crazy. If I knew that all the laughing and crying I did when I was young would appear like this, I wouldn't have laughed and cried so much in my life. At least this you should learn from me.

But, in serious, don't tell people about any of this, especially Lulú. Maybe she will need this program next year when she is officially a senior at fifty-five years. Let's hope El Obama is good and does not cut it. But yes, promise me, if Lulú sits in this chair, what I say never leaves here. You promise? OK, good.

If Lulú knew about José, she'd say, Tell him to leave his wife and make you a serious woman.

I've lived long enough. I know life is no movie. If José left his wife and got serious with me, you think he'd want to do exercise with me in the sofá the way he did all those years? I don't think so! He'd be like my brother Rafa. Who used to come home after work, park himself on the sofá in front of the TV, and drink until he fell asleep. Poor Miguelina. If she said something about it, he yelled at her, ¡Coño, mujer! Can you give me a few hours to relax? Miguelina was more alone than all of us because with each drink Rafa went more and more far away.

When I think of José's good wife, I think she's another Miguelina—aguantando. In the end, I got the best of that man. I never got the bad; only the sweet. We took good care of each other for many years. And you know what? José still comes to my apartment. Not like before. He closed his Everything Store after he had a stroke and scrunched up like a ciruela.

Ay, sorry. I swear to you, I don't talk my business. Here I vomit the words. I haven't been with a man since José. What was that, six years ago? It's crazy. Most women I know have closed their business down there. Unless they're keeping it secret.

You can tell me anything and it's secure with me.

Write that down: Cara Romero never shows the sausage to the pigs.

Lulú could never keep a lover a secret. Lulú is full of announcements. She takes a small thing, makes it big. I don't know anybody that likes to talk more than Lulú.

Many things Lulú says start with: Don't forget, if it wasn't for me . . .

In La Escuelita I always permitted Lulú to show off. Because she knows English really good. She reads in English, she writes good English, and was the first in our building to have a computer. This, she wants in the history books. So yes, in La Escuelita, Lulú talks and talks because she dique knows everything. But when I say something, people listen. This I learned from my father. The less you say, the more the people listen.

Let me give you one example: La Escuelita gave us the Metrocard with the map of the MTA. La Profesora put the map of the train on the wall and made círculos where La Escuelita was and all the places we could visit together: the Statue of Liberty, the Gardens Botánicos, the immigrant museum, the Museo de Arte, the zoo in the Bronx.

Where do you want to go first, Cara? La Profesora asked.

Ha! The look on Lulú's face when everyone turned to hear me. It was just like it was in the factory, people looked to me like I was in charge.

I said, I want to go to the Statue of Liberty.

So we went.

And let me tell you, it's not easy to get to the Statue of Liberty. We had to take the train and then the bus and then the boat and then walk and walk. It took us two hours. That's when I understood that New York is big. But big!

When La Profesora asked us if we wanted a special ticket to go to the crown, of course I said yes. And Lulú said yes. At first, almost everybody said yes. She said, there are many stairs to climb. For me, that's no problem. In our building the elevator breaks every time. You see the músculos on my legs?

Have you been to the statue? No? Only the tourists. Ha! We were tourists that day.

The statue was on an island. So big. When La Profesora

saw my open mouth she said, Wait until you see New York City when you go up to the crown.

With all the shit of life, it was nice to be the tourist.

We took the elevator to the feet of the statue. La Profesora showed us the picture of the 162 steps to get to the crown. Then, almost half of the group said they would wait on the bench. Including Lulú. She told everybody that the stairs were too much for me. For me, Cara Romero! Without asking, she pulled me to the bench to sit with her.

I want to see the crown, I said, and followed La Profesora to the stairs.

You do?

Yes, I do.

Pues, Lulú said, I was only staying down here for you because of your knees. ¡Vámonos!

Today I don't have pain in my knees, I said.

OK, Lulú said, we have to do one hundred sixty-two steps.

The steps were skinny and espiral. I looked to my feet and counted each step so I always knew where I was. I told Lulú, don't look up. It looks impossible but we can do it.

At forty-four steps, I asked Lulú if she wanted to take a break and she said no. When I got to seventy-five steps, that's when my legs started to burn, but because I do the exercises in the apartment where you go up and down like you're going to sit but you don't, I was still good. But I could hear Lulú breathing hard.

You OK?

Why you ask me that? Lulú said.

Lulú was in front of me. She was breathing so heavy, I pressed my hand on her back to support her.

Slowly, we arrived to the crown. Lulú was holding her stomach. I grabbed her arm and took her to look at New York City. Una belleza. We stayed there a long time, enough time for Lulú to breathe normal again. I could not feel my legs, but I was so happy to see all of the city with Lulú.

Cara Romero mira pa'llá. From Hato Mayor to the top of the Statue of Liberty.

OK, OK, fine, I will tell you about the interview. The lady was very nice. She was younger than me; not a lot, but with babies still. You know how the Americans are. They wait forever to have a baby and then have to fight like the devil to make it.

But OK, OK, she has a nice house, the lady. There were some plants that gave the house a little bit of life. And a painting, muy moderna, took all the attention in the room. I don't know if it was a blue frog or a blue elephant, maybe a cloud, maybe it was everything.

She needed me to work four nights every week. Sometimes five or six nights.

I travel a lot, she said.

¡Qué tristeza! Her children spend so much time with people they don't know.

Spanish only, she said.

Sí, claro, no hay problema, I said. She talked very fast and not like you or me: different. Like she had no air to breathe. When I am nervous I don't understand what the people are saying.

But I know I don't want to sleep in someone's house. How am I going to take care of La Vieja Caridad? And Ángela's children? What will Lulú do in the mornings if I sleep in this lady's house?

Yes, Lulú. I told you, she needs me. Last night she came to my apartment with the bottle of wine.

What am I going to do about Adonis? she asked and passed me a glass.

Apparently things are even worse with Adonis than we had imagined. He knew he was going to be laid off last year. Last year! And he didn't plan for it. He took that fancy cruise with the children anyway. His poor wife, Patricia, didn't have any idea of their problems. When he lost his job, he pretended to go to work for months.

Lulú is in a real crisis. You're not going to believe this. Or maybe you will because Lulú can be a little dramática. She took off her faja and threw it out of the window. This from a woman that puts on the faja from the moment she gets out of the bed. Always a size too small. She can't even bend to pick up something from the floor. Breasts high up on her chest, like missiles.

So imagine, poor Lulú at the window, wearing only her bata. When did she start wearing batas outside the house? I could see everything under there. I had never seen her stomach before, her tetas pointing to the floor.

I'll get it for you, I said, and rushed to the window to make sure the faja was down there. But it was gone. Disappeared. Who would take a faja from the street? Only in Washington Heights.

I could see the gray roots in her hair, half an inch of canas in the border of her forehead. I had no sense of how gray she was.

Lulú looks ten years older, maybe twenty years, with the fall of Adonis. For sure she hasn't eaten all week because she's emptied of life. How could mothers be happy when their children suffer? Impossible.

Maybe I don't always know what to say, but when I see her destroyed, I know living close to each other is important. On the phone, I could never see the new canas. Or her eyes, each one is like the mouth of a cave.

Why you can't find me a job where I can work in my apartment?

I still have five years before I can collect the Social Security. Lulú has seven years! It's impossible to live with only that money. Lulú and I had planned to work until seventy years old—the extra bonus in retirement was going to be for apartments in Miami. Or two small houses in Tampa. Or some other place, hot with beaches. One day, we thought, we could have more space, not on top of the other, to not hear everything through a heating tube. We would own houses across from each other so that we could wave hello from our front patios.

That dream is now far away. Now she's throwing fajas out windows.

¡Ay, Dios mío! We're gonna lose our apartments! Finish up on the streets! On that bench, in the park, feeding old bread to the pigeons!

We looked out of the window, seeing the night invade the streets, full of people going into the restaurants that sell un café for $4. A hamburger for $16. *Pfft!*

How am I going to help Adonis if I don't have any money? she asked.

I said, Let's drink the wine. I cooked dinner for us. Plátanos the color of the sun.

But like I told you, Mercury is in retrograde. That's what Alicia the Psychic said. So forget the next four weeks. Right now, Lulú doesn't want to hear that things will get better. She wants to cry, but she can't cry. So what does she do? She drinks more wine. She doesn't get the relief of crying. Ay, Lulú. Be strong, is all I can say. . . . You'll see, our next jobs will pay us double.

GENTRIFIED

RENT-STABILIZED BUILDING, INC.

BILLING INVOICE # 452906

Little Dominican Republic
New York, NY 10032

To: Cara Romero

INVOICE

MONTH RENT (MARCH 2009)	$888.00
OPEN BALANCE	$1,678.00
PAYMENT RECEIVED (03/10/2009)	−$250.00
LATE FEE:	$40.00

Remaining Balance: $2,356.00

Rent is due on the 1st of the month. Please pay rent on time to avoid late charges.

QUISQUEYA DENTAL

Washington Heights, NY

Service and Cost Breakdown

Patient:	Patient:	Acct. Number:
Cara Romero	654321	123456
Date: 04/18/2008	Periodontal Scaling and Root Planing per Quandrant	$182.00
Date: 07/30/2008	Periodontal Scaling and Root Planing per Quandrant	$182.00
Date: 11/18/2008	Periodontal Maint. Proc. (following active therapy)	$110.00

Amount Due: $474.00
Down Payment (30%): $142.20
Payment Plan Available:
5.9%–12% interest
12–24 month options available upon request.

JOB DETAILS

Full-time

Full Job Description:
Position: Security Guard, Middle School Grades 6–9
Location: The New York City Charter Middle School, Inwood, NY

Responsibilities:

- Monitor student entry and exit
- Deter and detect intruders
- Cafeteria duty to monitor and maintain order
- Receive and inspect all mail and packages
- Attend weekly meetings addressing current issues in the workplace
- Work overtime when necessary in order to cover parent-teacher conferences and student activities
- Answer and direct phone calls
- Encourage and ensure that students adhere to all school policies (uniforms, cell phones, IDs, etc.)
- Document unusual occurrences and collect witness statements
- Contact Police, Fire Department, or Emergency Medical Services (EMS) for emergencies

Qualifications:

- Must have security guard certification for both 8-hour and 16-hour class
- High school experience preferred but not required

- Ability to communicate effectively and often with parents and families
- Belief that all students can learn and achieve at high levels

Compensation:
Competitive and commensurate with experience and certification(s)

Interested candidates may send resume and cover letter to: NYC Charter Middle School. This is an equal opportunity employer and does not discriminate against any individual or group for reasons of race, color, creed, sex, age, national origin, marital status, sexual preferences, or mental or physical disability.

SESSION SEVEN

I have very good news for you today. Finally, Alicia the Psychic wrote to me and is talking about money. She said that in a month I will experience a big fortune. Maybe it's a job! And who knows what else. Because she said three things will happen. Three! Look, look, I asked Ángela to do a print for me in her oficina so you could see that Alicia the Psychic is not a robot.

Dear Carabonita,
I am so excited for you. Destiny has brought me into your life so I can deliver this wonderful news. Your guardians have sent me this message. After taking care of everyone, this is an opportunity to take care of yourself. Your fortune is waiting for you. You deserve a happy life.

Take note of this special date: four weeks from now your life will transform dramatically. Go to a calendar right now and write it down. What occurs on this day will start an irreversible change on your life path. This will be the first fortune. Then there will be two more. You have to believe me. I saw it very clearly in your future. I know we have not met in person, but I cannot stress enough how rare your circumstances are, Carabonita. The stars are working for you!

I believe you could see thousands of dollars during

this time. Can you envision a life with financial
security and love? I've been doing this for a long time,
Carabonita. I would not have bothered to write to you
if I wasn't absolutely certain that your life is about to
change.

I know you are having financial difficulties,
Carabonita, so I'm going to do something unusual.
I'm going to ask for less than many of my clients pay,
to help you out. Seize this opportunity. All I need is a
small fee to cover my essential equipment costs. And
it's completely risk-free!

I know my predictions sound too good to be true,
Carabonita, so I'm not asking you to take my word for
it. Put me to the test. And if for some reason my visions
have misled me, then I don't want your money. Just let
me know and I'll send you a full refund, no questions
asked.

One more thing. Don't feel guilty for the wonderful
things you're going to receive. Remember that no one
deserves this more than you.

Your friend and spiritual guide who loves you,
Alicia the Psychic

Does she sound like a robot to you? She knows that I
need the money and that I have sacrificed for others, making
sure everybody is OK. It's a big job. I showed this letter to
Lulú, but she said, It's a scam. It's a scam!

But the emails to me are very specific! Not just this one, all
of them. And even if I don't send her the money, she continues

to write to me. When Walter Mercado was on the TV every day—¡ay! it's terrible he is no longer on TV—he said something to me. OK, yes, to me and everybody watching the TV: that the people who have the vision have the responsibility to share what they see. Even if he wasn't on TV, Walter would have to go in the street and share the visions. It's a privilege to have this capacity. So I trust Alicia the Psychic, even if Lulú tells me I am crazy to trust.

But I am careful. I can smell scams.

For example, I received a request from a mother from Nigeria who had lost everything.

Help. Send money immediately, promise I will pay double, she said.

This Nigerian woman was alone with her children. Escaping from a violent man, the son of a king. She moved all the money he inherited from his father into a secret bank account, and she was the only one that knows the number. If you help me, I will share my fortune with you, she said.

The letter made me think of all the women, like me, that escape from men who are so crazy that in the middle of the night they chop the leg of another man. I had no secret money to hide when I left Ricardo. He didn't even have enough money to put gasoline in the moto. I left Hato Mayor with nothing, only Fernando and two or three things. But what I am trying to say is that a butcher and a prince have more in common when they are angry.

No, I didn't send the Nigerian woman money. I don't have the money. But I almost told her that I understand her life because I had to run too.

It's better to not respond. Because sometimes if you open

the door a little, the people move inside your apartment. You know what I mean?

La Vieja Caridad says I can make a good security guard. What do you think? And maybe I can be a guard in a school, because I'm so good to keep the children secure.

Like the other day. Ángela and I were walking with Yadiresela on Broadway. Ángela wants me to become a citizen because now the green card is like a tourist visa. We had many stops to make. The library. The photo studio to take a photo for my passport that expired many years ago. Before she leaves to Long Island she wants me to have all my papers organized.

Even if Mercury is in retrograde she received the loan she needed from the bank. But when she talks about Long Island she talks like she is going to la luna.

But OK, we were walking and this man I have never seen before was in front of the place for the hamburgers. You know the place—if you eat one, it's OK, but if you eat two, you shit in your panties? Oh, you know it? You like it? Ay. Every time, I get a stomachache.

But anyway, lots of strange people pass through this neighborhood because you can go to the George Washington Bridge very easy and get in the highway. Ángela and Yadiresela were walking and this man winked to Yadiresela and not to me. That was strange. Yadiresela is only ten years old. Una niña. The man was wearing a good suit of wool. His shoes were clean and fancy. His hands were manicured too. But I was suspicious.

Wow, you've grown, the man said to Yadiresela.

Do I know you? Ángela asked the man.

Let's go, I said, pulling Ángela. I felt the cold feeling behind my neck.

But Ángela, especially when I try to tell her what to do,
does the opposite.

You look just like your father, the man said.

Any idiota could see that Yadiresela looks like her father,
because of Ángela she has nothing.

You know Hernán? You work in the hospital? she said,
giving to the man all the information. All that education
made her a real pendeja.

Oh, but of course. Everybody knows Hernán, he said.

Can I take a photo of you, to show to my wife? the man
asked. She won't believe how much time has passed.

But I saw that the strange man wasn't wearing a ring.
Why talk about a wife? That doesn't smell bad to you?

I pulled Ángela's arm again.

Ay, Cara, what's wrong with you? she said.

Ángela and Yadiresela did a pose. Then another pose, like
they were modeling for a magazine.

Look, I don't care how nice this man looks. No man
should have a photo of Yadiresela, except her father.

What are you? Nine, ten? What's that, fifth grade?

He asked too many questions.

Sixth grade, Ángela said. She's very intelligent. And a
good singer. She has a solo at St. Rose of Lima next Sunday!

Do you see what I mean? Ángela with a spoon gave him
every information.

Oh, I know that church, he said.

While they're busy talking, I took out the camera that I
keep in my purse for exactly this reason and I took a photo
in case we need to make a Wanted poster.

After, I yelled to Ángela. Why are you teaching Yadiresela to talk to strange men on the street?

He knows Hernán, she said.

We don't know this, I said.

The next day, I went to Yadiresela's school and waited outside for her to come out. Ángela says it's OK for Yadiresela to walk home from school alone. I watch the news every day and I know that many things happen to girls that have ten years of age. Ángela thinks I am paranoica. She says we can't live thinking the worst, we have to think the best will happen. And maybe this works for her, because everything Ángela wants, she gets.

From the minute she arrived to New York, she said, I will be a professional. It took her seven years to finish the degree, but she finished con diploma. She said she wanted a good husband and two children and she now has Hernán. She said she wanted to buy a house and now she bought a house. She believes if you follow the plan, you can make everything happen. But I think you can work hard like me and have nothing. In this life you have to be lucky. I didn't send Alicia the Psychic some money, but I made a big circle on the calendar, like she said.

So, anyways. I followed Yadiresela from school. I know it's strange, but I didn't want her to see me following. Fernando didn't like it when I followed him. It created many problems with us. It humiliate him. But many things happen to boys too, so I did everything I could to keep Fernando secure. But it was not easy.

Imagine with Yadiresela. I am so connected to her. If something happened to her I would die. The day of the concert, I stood in the back of the church, close to the entrance,

to listen to her sing. Oh, one day you should go listen to her.
She is better than any of those singers on TV.

Anyway, I did not see the strange man, but it's possible he
saw me. He knows I took photos of him. So he has to be careful.

And you know what happened? That same week, on the
news, I saw that a young girl in this neighborhood had disappeared with the age of twelve. And later I saw the posters
in the streets.

WANTED: Information for MISSING PERSON.
Penélope González / Female / Black Hispanic /12 years
of age / DOB 05/01/1997 / 5'4 tall, weighing 110 lbs,
medium complexion, brown hair and brown eyes. She
was last seen wearing black sweats, black hoodie, and
sandals.

Not so different from Yadiresela. It happened only eight
blocks away from where we live.

And guess what? The reporter warned parents not to
share photos of their children on the computer. Especially
photos where you can see the school in the background. You
see? They said strange men take photos and put them on the
computer. They sell the girls. They only need to identify the
school. They watch and they grab and take them to another
state. They change their names so they disappear forever.

I don't care that Ángela calls me paranoica. She doesn't
understand that we live in a dangerous world with very sick
people. Somebody has to watch for the children.

Do you know the story about the monkeys paranoico?
No? I will tell you. My vecina Mariposa told me that the scientists see the monkeys from the jungle creating a big revolú

for the others. So they took them away temporarily, to study them so that they could eventually help the paranoid people. They gave them drugs so they were more calm. But you know what happened? When they came back to the community with the monkeys, everybody was dead or disappeared. And you know why? Because the community needs somebody like me to pay attention for the danger. Everybody cannot be calm. To be calm is a luxury!

So yes, if I take a job doing security in the school, I can sit and watch the cameras, and make sure the strange men never enter.

Ay, you're right! It's like when I watch Channel 15.

Recently I saw something on Channel 15 that can show you how much I care about the children and their safety.

Sabrina, the daughter of my neighbor, was in the lobby, around eleven in the night, wearing pajamas and shoes with pom-poms. In this cold weather! She was opening the door for one of her friends, who was wearing a Catholic school uniform. Then they disappeared off the camera. Maybe to smoke? Before, it was the boys we had to worry about. But the girls now are smoking like the boys. The next morning, I found loose tabaco all over the stairs.

Nothing happens in this building that I don't know. Sabrina's mother works two jobs so her daughter, dique intelligent, can go to Mother Cabrini. It's one of the good Catholic schools in the area. When she works in the night, she leaves her two daughters with the grandmother, who is forgetting things. If someone needs extra eyes and ears, it's Sabrina.

Why was the other girl still in the uniform, like she didn't have a house to go to?

When Fernando left I didn't sleep for many nights, thinking Fernando also stayed in lobbies like this one. Before I met Alexis, I worried. *What if Fernando sleeps on stairs and benches in the park like people without family? These children with the entire life in front of them, what if somebody makes them do disgusting things for a hamburger? That friend of Sabrina wasn't even carrying a backpack!*

So when I saw Sabrina appear in the lobby another night, and she disappeared from the camera with her friend again, I thought maybe I should talk to her. Sabrina needed to know that her activity was in the TV. I hadn't seen her in the camera letting in boys, just her little friend—but in a building where the bochinche travels she will get caught.

So I put on my coat, went down the stairs. I heard them laughing one floor down. Their voices louder and then suddenly everything got silent. Then that smell. Dios mío, that smell. They had been smoking la marijuana, like they didn't know that it made them not grow. The trap door to la heroína. It makes my heart break.

She's only una niñita and has to concentrate on school so she can get a good job with health insurance. Stay away from the drugs and drinking. That's all any mother wants. And Sabrina is pretty too. So pretty.

I walked down, close enough to see the girls holding hands. Then Sabrina got closer to the girl with the uniform. What are you doing? I wanted to say, but I couldn't talk. They kissed. On the mouth. And kissed again. Stop! I said, but maybe only inside my mind. Because they kissed more. I wanted to save Sabrina. What does she know about the world? She is ruining her life. Pero me tranqué. I told you, when I get nervous I lose the voice. They kissed like they were invisible to the world.

And I remembered that feeling, to kiss before knowing any bad, any evil. When I kissed with curiosity.

The girl with the uniform had her back against the wall, and when she opened the eyes, she saw me. She pushed Sabrina. They looked so scared of me. Of me!

I'm sorry, I said.

I dropped my keys, picked them up, and went back up the stairs. Maybe if I act like nothing happened, she can remain innocent. No, I don't plan to tell the mother what I saw. But Sabrina doesn't know this.

Why not? Ay. Maybe she will give Sabrina tremenda pela. Maybe with the baseball bat that she keeps by the door. I don't know. I think about Fernando. Now I see I could have been more gentle with him. I didn't understand this before he left. I learned the difficult way that you have to be gentle with your children, or you can lose them forever.

Ay, yes, I would like a Kleenex. Look what you do to me.

I don't know. I don't know what Fernando thinks of me. Still, every day I hope he will return to sit in my kitchen and eat my food. When he left, I asked the policía to help me find him. But they didn't help. Every time a person told me they saw him, I went looking for him como una loca. Not like my mother, that never looked for me.

I told you about the time where I went to the Bronx? Yes, when I met Alexis. I will confess to you. There was another time, before that. I don't like to think about it. Some things are too difficult to tell. But yes, a year after Fernando left, my neighbor Tita told me she saw him in the building on 180th and Pinehurst dique helping the super. Here I was, looking for him everywhere and then Tita tells me this. That he was only a few blocks away!

She said Fernando was wearing a knitted hat, but not the kind you buy on the street, but like someone made it for him, red with yellow flecks. Tita knits to relax so this is the first thing she noticed. But when he took off this hat she was surprised, because his hair was cut short on the sides, but on top, his hair sprung up and out, one big afro.

Like a rooster? I asked, and she said yes.

He looked healthy, not skinny. But the skin on the cheeks was not so good because maybe he was drinking too much milk and sugar. Fernando did love cereal with milk in the morning. He could eat one box for desayuno.

So, of course I went to see. And from outside I saw him in the lobby, holding a ladder for a man that was painting the wall. Imagínate mi corazón, I couldn't believe it.

Fernando! I yelled. I scared him because he let go of the ladder, the man fell down with the lata of the paint. Ay, Dios mío. What a mess. The man fell down on top of Fernando, gracias a Dios. But the paint was everywhere. I ran to them. The paint on the bottom of my foot made a more big mess.

Mami? he said. Ay, so many nights I didn't sleep, wanting for him to say that. The man asked, This is your mother?

Of course, we have the same nose. The same eyes. I was happy to hear his voice. Mami. Mami. Mami. It had been almost a year, he had left. One year!

Fernando had a tattoo in the wrist. An earring in the left ear.

Mami, what are you doing here?

I went close to smell him. He was OK. The whites of his eyes were bright and his pupils a normal size. He was OK. The skin, healthy. He was OK. Ay, that hurt. He was OK without me. Ay, what a relief. He was OK. He didn't look like a homeless.

Mami, leave, Fernando said. I have a mess to clean up.

With a calm voice, I asked him to come to dinner that night.

OK, he said.

He never came. He never called. And yes, he quit that job. Or maybe he was fired. I don't know. But when I went again, the super said Fernando told the authorities he didn't want to see me again.

What is wrong with this country? So cold. With a document, they ruin a life.

Ay, today I've talked too much.

TEMPORARY ORDER OF PROTECTION

DATE: Year of 2000 after Cara
went to look for Fernando
on 180th and Pinehurst
PRESENT: Honorable Judge

_____

In the Matter of a FAMILY OFFENSE Proceeding
Fernando Ricardo Romero
(Petitioner)
-against-
Cara Romero
(Respondent)

NOTICE: YOUR FAILURE TO OBEY THIS ORDER
MAY SUBJECT YOU TO MANDATORY ARREST AND
CRIMINAL PROSECUTION, WHICH MAY RESULT IN
YOUR INCARCERATION FOR UP TO SEVEN YEARS
FOR CONTEMPT OF COURT. IF YOU FAIL TO APPEAR
IN COURT WHEN YOU ARE REQUIRED, THIS ORDER
MAY BE EXTENDED IN YOUR ABSENCE AND THEN
CONTINUES IN EFFECT UNTIL A NEW DATE SET BY
THE COURT.

If you go after Fernando again you will go to jail. Punto final.

THIS ORDER OF PROTECTION WILL REMAIN
IN EFFECT EVEN IF THE PROTECTED PARTY

HAS, OR CONSENTS TO HAVE, CONTACT OR
COMMUNICATION WITH THE PARTY AGAINST
WHOM THE ORDER IS ISSUED. THIS ORDER
OF PROTECTION CAN ONLY BE MODIFIED OR
TERMINATED BY THE COURT. THE PROTECTED
PARTY CANNOT BE HELD TO VIOLATE THIS ORDER.

IT IS HEREBY ORDERED that CARA ROMERO observe
the following conditions of behavior:

Stay away from:

[A] Fernando Ricardo Romero

[B] the home of Fernando Ricardo Romero

[C] the place of employment of Fernando Ricardo Romero

Refrain from communication or any other contact by mail,
telephone, email, voice mail, or other electronic or any other
means with Fernando Ricardo Romero.

Refrain from assault, stalking, harassment, aggravated
harassment, menacing, reckless endangerment, strangulation,
criminal obstruction of breathing or circulation, disorderly
conduct, criminal mischief, sexual abuse, sexual misconduct,
forcible touching, intimidation, threats, identity theft, grand
larceny, coercion, or any criminal offense against Fernando
Ricardo Romero.

THE OFFICE OF
CHILDREN AND FAMILY SERVICES

In-Home Small Day-Care Application

Thank you for inquiring about starting an In-Home Small Day-Care Center. Operating a day-care center can be a rewarding professional decision. We are pleased to send you an application package. The Office of Children and Family Services encourages you to request help for additional technical assistance.

This package contains the information you will need to begin the application process. The Day-Care Center Required Documents checklist includes the thirty documents required to complete this application, including: fingerprint request form, criminal conviction statement, qualifications and references, emergency evacuation plan, report for water supply testing, first aid and CPR certification, behavior management training, menu planning, and a behavior management and child abuse policy for your small day-care center.

General Information

All applicants must be eighteen years of age or older and must complete this page

Please PRINT clearly

Applicant
Name: *Romero, Cara*　　**DOB:** *01/18/1953*
Address: *Washington Heights*
Do you speak English? *Yes*

Capacity Requested
Specify below the number of children, by age group, that you are requesting.
Number of Toddlers (18–36 months): 2
Number of Preschool (3 years–K): 2
Number of school-age (K–12 years): 2

Hours of Operation
Every day 7:00 a.m. to 7:00 p.m. is possible.

Director Qualifications
Levels of Education: *I did skool. I no my números and letras.*
Childcare Experience: *I am moder. I take kare of Ángela y Hernán's 3 children.*

Qualification of Typical Duties of Day-Care Staff

- Lifting and carrying children
- Desk work
- Driver of vehicle
- Food preparation
- Facility maintenance
- Evacuation of children in an emergency

References

Reference #1. *Lulú Sánchez*
Reference #2. *Hernán Ortiz*
Reference #3. *Ángela Romero Ortiz*
To the best of my knowledge, the statements that I have provided in this application are true and accurate.

Signature:

_____

THE OFFICE OF
CHILDREN AND FAMILY SERVICES

In-Home Small Day-Care Application
Behavior Management (Discipline) Plan

Acceptable Methods

- Focus on Do rather than Don't. For example, "Let's choose a better word" instead of "Don't say that."
- Redirect. In a conflict, distract with an alternate toy or activity.
- Offer choices: "You can either sit on the floor or at the table to play."
- Praise positive behavior: "Thank you for putting away the toys!"
- Listen to the children and respond to their needs before trouble starts; keeping the children busy helps prevent conflict.
- Children learn by example: Use please and thank you.

PROHIBITED

- Corporal punishment is prohibited. Shaking, slapping, twisting, squeezing, and spanking.
- The use of room isolation is prohibited. No child can be isolated in an adjacent room, hallway, closet, darkened area, play area, or any other area where a child cannot be seen or supervised.
- Food cannot be used or withheld as a punishment or reward.

I,_____ agree to comply with the Behavior Management Plan.

Signature:

_____

SESSION EIGHT

¡Ay, look! You have a glass of water ready for me? Today, I didn't even have to ask. Ha! You must want to get to work right away. Yes, I understand we don't have much time left together and you want me to get a job soon. And that is very good, because I need a job. But I don't think taking care of children in my apartment is a good idea for me. No.

Did you see how many papers it is? A bible of papers. I thought for many hours about this possibility and decided—no.

It's true that sometimes the new people that live in the building ask me if I could take care of their babies. And it's true that I want to work from the apartment, but after what happened to me this week, I say no. No, y no, y no. I can do it, but not officially. I don't want to get in trouble with the authorities or have problems with the people.

OK, let me explain.

I'll start with poor Lulú. The situation with Adonis is destroying her. She was more fat than me, but now she's empty, her clothes dancing on her. It's terrible. I try to make her eat, but she has lost her appetite. Her hair, like una vieja and now you only see the canas. It's another Lulú. If only I had the money to pay for her to go to the salón I would make her do it.

Lulú, in front of me, tries to be strong. But in the night I hear her laments traveling through the tube in my kitchen.

The problem is that in the beginning Adonis thought they could temporarily rent a place until he finds a good job, but his wife Patricia confessed to Lulú that every day she learns of something else Adonis bought with credit and never paid. Every day there is a bill. For example, the school of the children, that he didn't pay for many months. Patricia trusted Adonis because he has a financial degree from one of the best schools in the country, but now they are in big trouble.

Of course, Lulú feels responsible. I understand this. A children's mistake is a mother's responsibility. Lulú told them they can live with her until they find their feet, but Adonis, because he's especial, said he will never return to Washington Heights. Never.

I don't make opinions. I hold Lulú's hand. I let her desahogarse in my kitchen. Lulú can't cry but, like I told you, she talks and drinks wine to undrown.

But the point is that this week Adonis left the children with Lulú for many, many days. He told Lulú he can't look for a job if he has the children to care for in the apartment. And Patricia has to work every day. Even Saturday. In the past Lulú would go to their apartment for a few hours to stay with the children. For a few hours it was easy. But now that they stay with her, she is destroyed. Patricia has a long list of rules that Lulú has to follow, punto final.

No bobo.

No leche before bed. No leche, not even water, outside the schedule.

No saying no!

Lulu can't say no to the children, never. Or make an angry

face when the three-year-old makes pictures on the wall. Patricia and Adonis are worse than Ángela, who try to control
everything. Not even Ángela has so many rules.

No pela.

No sleeping on the stomach.

No salsa, merengue, bachata. No radio. Punto final.

Only música clásica. Patricia gave Lulú CDs to stimulate
the brain of the babies. And only organic fruits—unless the
skin is thick, like aguacate or piña or toronja. And you know
it's impossible to find organic fruits in Washington Heights.
It's expensive. But even in the crisis, she says: only organic
food.

No TV. Never. Adonis covered the TV in Lulú's apartment
with a sheet. It's true that the eighteen-month-old is very intelligent and knows to talk with his hands. He can tell us if
he wants leche or water, if something tastes good, if he wants
more.

Lulú doesn't complain about the children or Patricia di-
rectly. Patricia is working six days a week in the lawyer's office so Adonis and the children have something to eat. She is
the only one making money. And Lulú raised Adonis to be
too nariz pará; he would never be like that lawyer that went
to work in Wendy's. But that is exactly what Adonis should
do. But I don't make opinions.

The point is that I read this application to start the day
care, and I am confident I can lift and carry the babies. I can
prepare food. I can maintain a clean place for the children to
sleep, play, and eat. You already know I am very good for the
emergency. I can maybe even learn how to drive, but in New
York I don't think it's necessary. And I don't know what is

desk work ? But, OK. I am sure I can do it. But the Behavior Management Plan, no. Not with children that are not my blood. No way.

Let me explain. I am good with babies. When Yadiresela was born, Ángela was not ready to have children. But Hernán wanted the children. Many children. If it was his decision, they would have a baseball team. He had ten years more than Ángela and he was ready to start a family. She wanted to study and to be a professional. She wanted to make money for her house. She did not want to go pa'trás como el cangrejo like many married women. She wanted to progress. She would talk about how the scientists make proof that the people who make benefit from marriage are the men. The wife die early and get sick, she said. The husband, the opposite.

If it wasn't for Hernán being so good and persistent, Ángela would have not married. It's like he said to Ángela, Let me be your wife.

So of course, even though he sweats la gota gorda working in the hospital, when Yadiresela was born Hernán gave her food, changed the diaper, and put her to sleep almost every day. This, even when Ángela took some months off from work to dique take care of the baby. And Ángela knows how to cook, but she says, Ay, Hernán, I like it better how you do it. Then she plays with his ear and rubs his back and, just like La Vieja Caridad 's dog, Fidel, he turns over, shows his belly, and that's it, he gives in to her.

But Yadiresela was not an easy baby. And Hernán was good, but not a mother. She cried constantly. Every day from 4:00 to 6:00 p.m. Yadiresela cried. A good time too, because it was exactly when I finished doing work in the factory. The van left me home at 3:50 p.m. I had ten minutes to change my clothes and, like a clock, Yadiresla would cry—but cry!

She was born soon after Fernando left. So when she cried I felt the crying inside of me. So I carried Yadiresela like I carried Fernando. The crying was too much for Ángela. The minute I arrived Ángela gave me the baby and go into her room to sleep. If it was her decision, she would go back to work in the office immediately, but Hernán didn't want the baby to be with strange people all day. Not when she was so little. In the night, Ángela wanted to continue to go to the school.

So, for Hernán, it's good I was in the building to help them. It's good that we live like we have one house together, in two different apartments. When I stayed with Yadiresela, I turned on the public TV to the documentaries because they are relaxing. I learn a lot. One of them was about babies in Brazil that were abandoned by their mothers. You know this one? No? Ah. To make the baby more calm, the women take off their shirt and put the baby touching their skin. So when Yadiresela cried, I made her naked and put her inside my blusa. It made her stop crying every time. This is why Hernán has a soft spot for me. Because for many, many months I bring the silence to the house. I needed the silence too.

The skin on the skin method worked.

Write that down: Cara Romero is good with the children.

Even with difficult babies like Yadiresela. But I controlled her behavior so good that now when she finish eating, she wash her plate. She is so intelligent, the teacher moved her from fifth grade to sixth grade in the middle of the year. All these good things I did without Ángela's books.

Yes, Ángela has a mountain of books from the library. Dique to be a better mother, but what she means is a better mother than me. She thinks I give pelas to her children. But I never give pelas to her children. Only pao-pao on their hand when they don't listen. And sometimes a little slap in the leg with my hand. Never a pela.

When Fernando left and didn't come back, Ángela became nervous that maybe her children will abandon her too. She said, We can't make the same mistake of our mother. But we are not like Mamá, who was very cold. She never hugged us or told us that she loved us. We tell our children we love them and hug them all the time.

You have to understand: Ángela, even if she wanted to, can't hire a babysitter because it's too much money. So we try to resolver. Since I lost my job in the factory, I have more responsibilities with the children. I help to make food for them, pick up Yadiresela in the bus stop, pick up Milagros in the day care. Before I lost my job, they had to pay $10 an hour to la vecina to do many of these things. But la vecina did not also cook the children dinner, wash their clothes, and clean the apartment.

Do they pay me money now? No. They give me some money to buy la compra and to pay for my utilities. That's OK, because we are family and I love the children.

What I'm trying to tell you is that the American children get traumatized more easy than us.

Ah, OK. Yes. I will tell you what happened so you can understand. You know Lulú has to take care of her grandchildren, and for me it's easy to take care of the babies and cook for everybody, but for Lulú, not so much. So I have to help her. Taking care of the children has destroyed Lulú. Destroyed! So I invite her to my apartment with the babies. And it's good because Ángela wants Milagros to have playdates with other children, like Lulú's grandchildren. They are very intelligent because they are from Brooklyn. And Ángela loves Brooklyn. She says playdates help develop emotional intelligence. So Lulú and I put the children together and see them become more intelligent while we drink wine.

But Julio, who is five, cannot play with the babies. He is a tsunami because, when he pulls Yadiresela's hair, Ángela doesn't give him a chancletazo. She takes a deep breath, touches his shoulders, looks him in the eyes, and says: Julio, it is not nice to pull your sister's hair.

Of course, Julio knows it's not nice. Julio was born not nice. He likes to bite. He likes to hit. He was born making the trouble. Some children have this character. They are born like that. Punto final.

But Ángela tries to do like the Behavior Management Plan in this application. She does the redirection.

Julio, let's choose another way to get your sister's attention. Julio, let's not hit your sister. Julio, we are all friends.

You know what happens next? Julio pulls Yadiresela's hair even more hard!

And then—¡el colmo!—Ángela tries dique to stay calm and says, Julio, if you don't say sorry to your sister, I'll give you a time-out.

A time-out!

You know what happens? Julio does not say sorry. Then,

Ángela sits him in a chair in another room and says, Julio, you can't get up until you understand what you did wrong.

Pfft!

She talks to Julio like he has the capacity to control himself. Not even his pipí he controls. My son, Fernando, never dared to make pee in the bed the way Julio does. At five years old, Julio makes pee in the bed every night! Mira, I would spank that mala costumbre out of him. It would only take one good spank in the nalga, not hard—he won't even remember when he is an adult. Just enough so he knows to respect and not to pee in the bed. If Ángela would let me discipline Julio, he would be a good boy and do what we say, like Yadiresela.

So yes, last week I thought, *Maybe I already have a day care except I don't get paid. So to have a day care in my apartment would be a good job for me.* But Julio tested my patience.

No, nothing. Listen to me, everything was OK. The babies were becoming more intelligent together, Yadiresela was doing her work for the school on the sofá. Julio was playing with his dolls of superheroes. I put the dinner of spaghetti with tomato sauce on the table. I went to the kitchen for one minute, one minute, and Julio, I don't know why, took the plate of spaghetti and threw it on top of the babies.

Lulú screamed. The babies cried. Yadiresela yelled, ¡Tía!

I ran from the kitchen, and you won't believe it—spaghetti sauce everywhere: on Lulú's shirt, all over the babies, on Julio's hands.

Immediately we checked the babies. They were OK,

because I always rinse the pasta with cold water, so it's never too hot. And the sauce was at the temperature of the room. Gracias a Dios.

¡Mi blusa! Lulú cried.

I yelled, Julio! And he ran around the apartment, laughing.

Please, Julio, I said, and grabbed him around his stomach. He kicked and kicked and escaped from my arms. This is where I'm different from my mother. I remembered Ángela's instructions. I breathed. And I practiced behavior management.

Please, Julio, I said. Cálmate. Stop, Julio, or I will give you a time-out.

He looked to me and laughed. Laughed in my face! ¡Malcriado, coño!

So I took him, picked him up, and I shook him like a maraca. Squeezed his arms, hard. And I yelled, ¡Coño, maldito muchacho, ¿tú quieres un chancletazo?! Julio started to cry hysterically.

In that moment, Ángela arrived. She saw everything. Mami! Mami! Julio screamed.

She ran to me and took Julio away from me.

It was so dramatic, like he was being saved from a monster. But they were just words. I would never hurt Julio. If I ever hurt Julio, Ángela would never forgive me. So never.

He hugged Ángela's neck very tight and cried like a baby.

What's wrong with you? she yelled at me.

Me?

Then she looked to Julio and said, Mi amor, I know Tía is scary sometimes. It's OK, Mami is here. Yadiresela, get Milagros. We're going home, Ángela said.

She looked to me and screamed, You are just like Mamá! No, you are worse! You will never take care of my children again. Never! And she slammed the door.

Yes, thank you, I need more water. It's very dry in here. Yes, I am upset. Every time I hear that door slam it's like it is 1998 again, when Fernando left and never came back. My heart beats fast, my chest hurts, and I have to sit down because my sugar falls.

In the past, when I felt that way, I thought I was dying. But then Lulú taught me the trick about how to calm down. You know the trick? Say three things you see, three things you hear, and then move three parts of the body.

Window, Table, Plant. Refrigerator, clock, ambulance. Fingers, toes, jaw.

Anyway, I try not to think about the past, because what can we do about it?

We all commit errors, but Ángela is not fair to me.

Ángela is angry all the time for something. Like she wants to make me disappear. She wants to make Mami, Papi, Rafa, Hato Mayor disappear too. If Hernán didn't have the job in the hospital, she would move far away to Boston, Tampa, Yonkers, anywhere but Washington Heights. She hates everything about the neighborhood. She spits on it and says it's so dirty, so loud, so crowded, so stinky. Every day she has a complaint. Soon she will leave us and move to Long Island.

She doesn't care about me. She made all her plans and never asked if it was OK with me. I don't have a car. How will I see the children? I swear, maybe I should disappear forever? Maybe then she would appreciate me.

Of course, it hurts. After everything I have done for her
and her children, she treats me this way. After all I have suffered in my life . . .

Ay, what must you be thinking about me!

You are so young. How many diplomas do you have?
Your mother must be really proud of you. Look at you, with
a good job like this. I bet you get good benefits. And a good
pension. You are set for life.

Ángela is set for life. She has a retirement account. She has
Hernán. She is getting her house. But me? What do I have?

I'm sorry. You are so nice to me. It's that everybody asks,
Cara, cook for me. Cara, clean for me. Cara, pick up the children. Cara, do this mandado for me. Cara. Cara. Cara. But
who will take care of me? Not even my mother, my own
mother, took care of me. If people only knew . . .

You want to know? You really want to know? OK, I'll tell
you.

After Ricardo cut off the leg of Cristián, I ran to my mother's house in the middle of the night, one mile with a baby
and my bag. I was terrified. I tried to open the gate, but it
was locked. I yelled and yelled to open the gate.

Fernando was heavy. The heat was like an oven. The mos-
quitoes were eating me alive. Ángela, who had thirteen years,
came to the window to look, but she could do nothing. Then
Mamá opened the door and came outside.

What did you do? she said.

Mamá, open the gate.

Go home.

Mamá, please, I begged.

Go home to your husband. He's a good man, she said.

Mamá, I can't go back to him. He's going to kill me.

Maybe you deserve it, she said and went back inside. She dragged Ángela away from the window.

Mamá left me to sleep outside on a plastic chair, like a homeless. Do you know what it feels like to have a mother sending you back to that salvaje? How long that night was for me? In the dark, alone, with Fernando on my chest?

After many hours, Ángela unlocked the gate. We went into the bedroom, very silent, and went to sleep.

The next day, Mamá found me and Fernando in Ángela's bed. She pulled Ángela arm and threw her off the bed. ¡Coñazo! ¡Hija de la gran puta! You don't respect me?

Ángela ran to the sala. Mamá grabbed her by the hair and Ángela kept trying to get away. She trapped her in the corner on the chair and with Papá's belt she beat her almost to death. Ángela did not cry, holding her tears. Of course this made Mamá more angry. I was paralyzed, holding Fernando. I wanted to jump on her and pull her off of Ángela that had thirteen years . . . almost the same age like Yadiresela. Una niña. But I couldn't move. My father heard the gritos from the other side of the house, and pulled Mamá away to make her stop.

Mamá turned to me and said, This is your fault.

Do you see how I suffered?

And yes, Ángela suffered too. But I didn't want that to happen. I was hurting too. I didn't know if Cristián was dead or alive. I only knew that Ricardo was too macho to forgive. If it wasn't for my father that convinced Mamá to let me stay, I would be dead.

Yes, of course I'm grateful that my sister had the courage

to open the gate, of course! You don't have to ask me that. And I promised Ángela many times—many, many times, when she was healing from the pela Mamá gave her—that I was going to help her come to New York. And I kept the promise. But still, Ángela is very angry with me.

You have to believe me. I am nothing like my mother.

I don't remember us having time to play or eat together when we lived in Hato Mayor. But in New York, when Fernando was still with us, we all eat together like a family. We watched the TV in the kitchen and laughed almost every night. When Ángela or Hernán eat with us, it was good because Fernando and Ángela had a strong connection. When they talked in English about TV or a music, I didn't understand the English, but I laughed when they laughed.

I was never cruel like my mother. Or cold to the children.

OK, sometimes Fernando and I had fights, but little fights. Like when I didn't let him close the door of his room. He wanted privacy. I told him, I pay the rent, I make the rules. The door stays open. Anyways, what secrets could he have from me? He was in his room all day, listening to the music. I left him alone. It was not a problem. The only thing I asked was: clean the toilet, throw out the garbage, clean the dishes, and do good in the school.

Ay, wait, if you permit me, I need to get more water. Thank you.

Look, I committed some errors. But the day he left was an accident.

Yes, an accident. It was Sunday. I was ironing the clothes. It's the only day I had to do all my oficios. Fernando was eighteen. He graduate from the high school, and wanted to go outside to be with his friends. And, like I told you, it was very dangerous in the streets, and he was dressed in a funny way. How? You know what I mean. The pants were too small for him. You could see everything. I mean—everything. You understand?

Change your pants, I said.

I had a mountain of clothes this high. I had to iron all of it. I had a migraine. In those days I had many migraines. The pain in my eye, like a knife.

They're fine, Mami, he said and went to open the door.

People will get the wrong idea, I said.

C'mon, Mami, I'm already late.

You want the building to talk about you? You know how that makes me look?

How it makes *you* look?

Yes. You know how it makes me look.

Oh my fucking God, he said, and walked around the sala like a bull trapped in an arena. The nose flared, the feet hitting the floor. But I couldn't let him go out like that.

¡Coñazo! I said. Listen to me or—

Or what? he yelled. He had never talked to me like that before. His voice got deep and loud, his arms stretched out like this, and he started punching the air. And right there, I saw Ricardo in his face. The same face, the same hands. All the times Ricardo would raise his voice with me and hold me by the neck and lift me in the air.

Look, one day you are big and the baby is small, and then the next day the baby is big, much more big than you, much more strong.

Fernando! I will tell you one more time: you can't leave the house like that.

And you know what he did? I am holding the iron and I said, Don't open the door, Fernando. But he opened it. Like I was invisible. Una cualquiera.

So I threw the iron to the door to stop him.

The iron hit the side of his face. Fernando fell to the floor and made a grito so loud. I am sure everyone in the building could hear.

But why did he get in the way?

Of course, I ran to him.

You're fucking crazy! he yelled.

I laughed with relief. Yes, laughed. I could have killed him but, gracias a Dios, no. He was OK. I saw blood come down the side of his face, but he was moving toward the bathroom.

Ay, Dios mío. Let me look.

Get away from me! he yelled.

I ran to get some napkins with some ice.

Don't be dramático, I said. It doesn't look bad.

But he pushed me, stood up, and went to the bathroom.

Tell me you are OK, I asked him from outside the bathroom door, the ice burning my hands.

Leave me alone, he said.

I waited outside the bathroom for a long time. The ice melt and I couldn't feel my hands. Many times I said, It was an accident. I never want to hurt you, but he said nothing. When he finally came out and walked to his bedroom, I saw the cut on his face—it was bad, but not so bad. I was lucky. He was lucky.

Later, when I thought he was sleeping, I heard the door slam. *Prá!* The door slammed hard and definite. I thought he left for a few hours. But he never returned.

Why are you looking to me like that? Please don't look to me like that. I love my son so much. Where's the water?

GENTRIFIED

RENT-STABILIZED BUILDING, INC.

BILLING INVOICE # 453074

Little Dominican Republic
New York, NY 10032

To: Cara Romero

INVOICE

MONTH RENT (APRIL 2009)	$888.00
OPEN BALANCE	$2,356.00
PAYMENT RECEIVED (04/23/2009)	−$193.00
LATE FEE:	$40.00

Remaining Balance: $3,091.00

Rent is due on the 1st of the month. Please pay rent on time to avoid late charges.

SESSION NINE

Ay, I'm sorry. Please forgive me. I didn't sleep the entire week.

Why? Because every week more problems. Ángela will still not talk to me. She's an Aries. It takes a very long time for an Aries to forgive. I tried to reach her, yes, by phone. I knocked on her door, but she refused to talk.

Yes, I apologized to Ángela. I tried to make peace with her—ay, how I tried.

I made her the pastelitos with raisins! And I hate the raisins. But for her, I put the raisins. You know what she did? She left them in a bag, hanging on the door of my apartment! Gracias a Dios for Hernán that understands that everybody has a bad moment. Everybody commits an error. Ángela acts like I didn't raise those children too. But Hernán knows what I have done for those children and even when Ángela is angry, he takes care of me.

You know what he did? He came to my apartment and said, Get dressed.

Learn this from me: Sometimes when you can't change your ánimo you have to have people like Hernán to remind you about the important things in life. Sometimes we need help to not drown in a glass of water.

Yes, I know, I have real problems. But it's good to have people to remind us that we have survived a lot more than this.

So I got dressed and Hernán drove me to City Island. Yes,

it was hot enough to sit outside. I took my shoes off and put my feet inside the water. It was like ice. But I needed something. Do you ever have that feeling? When you need something to wake you up? And we saw the sky turn orange, and ate un montón—a box this big—of camarones fritos with cold cervezas.

Sometimes life feels very small and other times it feels very rich. And when it feels small I think it's because I don't let myself, you know, enjoy the life.

It reminds me of when I would go to La Escuelita and La Profesora opened the can with cookies.

Try one, she told me.

Lulú took many of them. But I was suspicious. Nobody gives free cookies for nothing. But La Profesora insisted, Cara, eat the cookie.

I ate the cookie.

Oh my God, those cookies! Why are they so good?

What I am trying to tell you is that last week I said too much, but I need you to understand that I am not a bad person.

Yes, bad things happened. But, listen to me, life was very difficult in Hato Mayor. Yes, Mamá y Papá are complicated people, but they worked hard to take care of us. We were poor but never hungry. And Papá even had a good plan for me. I was going to live with mi tía in la capital to study in the university to become a professional. He wanted all his children to have the capacity to express themselves. He didn't talk very much, but on Sundays people came from everywhere to dictate tonterías to my father so he could write their letters.

He said, A talent with words is better than a few dollars in your pocket.

But I didn't go to la capital to study. I went with Ricardo.

Ricardo loved my stories, called me his little cotorrita. Fast, fast we fell in love. In that time, so many men came after me. But Ricardo had pockets full of treasures. One day he gave me a gold bracelet, thin like a thread, so shiny. The next year, I embarrassed. Of course, my mother obligate him to marry me with papers. She said, My baby will not be sin padre.

In the beginning, Ricardo was not bad. Like I told you, it was better than living with my mother, because she had a temper like the devil. Ricardo had a good job, his own butcher kiosko in the market, where people came from everywhere to get his meat. He owned a little land too, and raised many animals. What did I know about men? I was nineteen.

He was sweet when I was embarrassed. Yes, embarrassed, with a baby in my stomach. The correct word is pregnant? OK, I was pregnant. And he was very sweet with me. So this makes me think he really loved me. There was no antojo he wouldn't get. He massage my feet in the night like una masa de pan. All the women in the barrio said he was bitten good by my brown eyes and my big nalgas. And for a time, we ate meat almost every day. Who can say that in Hato Mayor? Nobody! And not like the meat here, that is more dead than dead. The meat was fresh and like nothing you have ever put in your mouth.

What? No, that was not Fernando. That baby never came.

We tried again and I lost another baby. And this I know frustrated Ricardo. If I was an animal on his farm, he would have killed me and cooked me for dinner. I was not his cotorrita anymore. For a long time, he didn't look to me. My mother gave me the botellas full of herbs to force the fertility. She said he was going to leave me for another woman if I didn't give him a baby. But, between us, I wanted him to leave. To live with Ricardo was not easy.

So, of course, my mother thought her botella worked the miracle when I got pregnant at twenty-six years old. That is old in Hato Mayor. Here, in New York, women have babies at forty, even fifty years! And the sweet Ricardo I first met appeared again. So I acted like the wife and I permitted him to be the man. One of my talents is to make people happy.

And when things were good, I knew all the ways to make him happy. That's right. Exactly what you think. Yes, we did it in every corner of the house. He was always sticking it in me. I was washing the dishes, he stuck it in me. I was about to go to sleep, he stuck it in me. And he's not a small man. And when he used the father voice with me, ay, call the bomberos! I smell smoke!

But everything changed when Fernando was born, who came early and fast. I knew Fernando was coming because he kicked and kicked in my stomach like somebody knock on the door. I prepared everything: the clean towels, the soap, and the five gallons of water, purified. And the night Fernando came, everything fell on me at the same time. The cramps, the pain in my back, my stomach dropped. But I thought I had more time because my fountain was not broken. So I didn't wake up Ricardo. To be alone was easier. I liked the silence of the night.

I walked around our casita with two rooms. I made it

very nice: one wall was yellow and the other wall was pink. And Ricardo painted the floor of cement the color of grass. Because does not green make you happy too? Yes. It's my favorite color.

I was tired, but the pain was not too much. So I lay back down in the bed. And Ricardo breathed more loud than that train that passed our house every day. I even fell asleep. And then, you know how Fernando slammed the door and never returned? How he went away without warning me? Without giving me the time to stop him or put sense in his head? That's exactly how Fernando came into the world. *Prá!* He woke me up with pain. The pain more intense every minute. So I kicked Ricardo. Wake up! I said. Get the Old Woman Who Knows.

The Old Woman Who Knows bring many babies into the world. She never lost a mother. You know how many women and babies don't survive? With umbilicals tied around their neck. Born with feet first. Or because the mother has an infection. So many things can go wrong. But not for the Old Woman Who Knows. She did all my examinations and knew more than the fancy machines in the hospitals in New York. She looked to my stomach, because it was round and high, she knew: It's a boy! She showed me where the nalgas and feet were.

Eat more protein, she said. If not, he'll be too small.

So I did.

Stop with the chicharrones, she said. If not, the baby will rip you.

So I did.

She even taught me how to have the baby alone, if necessary.

Ay, the pain! I made noises like the cows when they're in suffering, low and deep. I sense the vibrations of my voice inside my chest. But Ricardo didn't wake up. I pulled the sheets from him. He smelled heavy of rum and beer.

I kicked Ricardo hard in his back with my heel. Nothing. The sun was already coming from the windows.

I kicked him again, even more hard. He fell to the cold cement floor.

¡Coño! he yelled, ready to fight me. Then he understood what was happening.

Go! I yelled. Tell the Old Woman Who Knows to hurry.

Ricardo was shaking like a leaf.

I stood up and pushed my back against the wall. It hurt. Ay, Dios mío, it hurt. I had seen many women have babies. But they had time to rest. Not me. My son didn't wait for the Old Woman Who Knows. Ricardo was putting on his shoes when I felt it: Fernando's head was right here. You see here, where the bones are, between the legs? Imagine having a creature stuck inside there.

I felt like an animal. I got low, close to the floor, my legs open, como cagando.

¡Ayúdame! I yelled.

I'll be right back, he said.

No! You can't leave now. Get the towels. Get the water. Hurry!

He put the towels next to me and stood there, paralyzed.

So, who had to catch Fernando alone? This one here. And this will tell you a lot about me. Some people forget what to do in a moment like that, but me, I remembered.

Write that down: Cara Romero is good under stress.

When I felt the head, I knew how to push to make it come out: Patience. Don't push hard. Give the body the time to do the work. Trust the body. Push when you feel the ganas. First the head. Then the shoulders.

Just like that, Fernando slipped out of me, like when my hands are wet and I hold a soap. I cleaned the nose, the mouth, and the eyes. And when I heard him cry. ¡Ay santo! Nothing more amazing than that first cry. And he glued onto my teta immediately and soon after that my belly emptied, and there was Ricardo looking to everything inside of me that spill to the floor.

Everything.

And my son, a beauty. Un morenito with a head full of hair. All fingers in the hands and the feet.

Go! I said. Go get her now!

And he did. And that was good because I wanted to be alone with Fernando. Ricardo was useless. He proved that.

After Fernando was born, I lived with Ricardo two years. You know, I thought he was going to be happy, because finally he had a son. But no, he was difficult with me. If the sancocho I made was too salty, he accused me of being distracted. He got angry when the chickens didn't produce eggs. He became more jealous. He made many excuses so I didn't leave the house. He didn't like the neighbors and got angry when I talked to them. He said he needed my help in the kiosko, with the animals, with the land—so I was always with him. Food and shit is the life of an animal. So food and shit was my life with Ricardo.

I was not his little cotorrita. I was the mother of his son. Punto final.

With or without what happened to Cristián, in the end, I would have left. There is only so much a woman can take.

No, I didn't return to Hato Mayor for a long time.

For so many reasons. I was too busy. I didn't have money. And, of course, Fernando.

It's strange because in those years I never thought I was afraid to return, but talking with you makes me think I was trying to protect him.

Look, the one time Fernando met his father he had sixteen years. It had been over ten years since we were in Hato Mayor.

For many years Ángela, Rafa, and I sent money to help our parents make the house more modern. The idea was that if we visited we could be more comfortable. But nothing ever worked. You know how they work over there. Oh, you don't know? You have never ever traveled to the Dominican Republic? Interesting. Well, let me tell you.

To flush the toilet, you had to get the pail of water from the tinaco in the patio. Imagine, me, with my nose that is so sensitive. Forget Fernando, so gringo. I would tell him, Throw the toilet paper in the basura, not the toilet. But did he ever remember? He made poo and left it there for somebody to take care of. I was humiliated.

It was so hot. The humidity you can't imagine; the sheets in the bed always wet. We only had a small fan attached to the window. But it was nice to share the room with Fernando. In New York he was in his room all the time. In Hato Mayor he stayed outside and also close to me.

We went to Hato Mayor together because my mother

said she was sick. On the phone she complained that her tetas felt pain, but she didn't want to go to the doctor.

From the night to the morning, she said. I've been emptied. I'm so skinny.

Get an exam of the blood, Mamá.

I have this fatigue that doesn't go away.

Por Dios, make an appointment!

Ay, Cara. I'm only old. When you get to my age you'll see.

The point is that I made the trip to see if she was dying or no. Getting flaca and having pain in the tetas is not good. I tell you this because you are young and women have to be careful for the cancer. Do you check every year for the cancer? Yes? Good.

If Mamá was not going to the doctor to check I had to go and see if I can smell the cancer on her. You know, the cancer smells like the water of the sea.

When I got there, Mamá did not smell like the sea. And she was not flaca. Of course, she tricked me!

Everybody came by to say hello, to put the nose in the maletas and see if we carried presents for them. Fernando was in the patio all the time. Inside the house there was nowhere to sit. Family tried to take him on the moto to the centro to hanguear. But he did not want to go. In New York Fernando was not afraid to be in the streets. He begged me to go out all the time. In Hato Mayor, Fernando was not so curious. He jumped when he heard the truck make loud sounds. He stepped back when primos came close to look at his sneakers and new jeans. Still, everything was going OK until Ricardo appeared.

Buenos días, Ricardo said through the iron gate, smiling.

I felt a rock inside the chest when I heard his voice. A rock the size of a fist.

Mamá ran to open the gate for him.

I had to remember that I took care of myself. I had a job. That I raised my son alone. That he had no power over me.

What are you doing here? Papá said. He understood that Ricardo should not be there.

Pero ven acá, Ricardo said. Can't a father see his son?

Mamá pointed to the plastic chair Fernando was sitting on, the same one I sat on outside the gate the night I left Ricardo. She said, Ricardo, this is your son.

Oh, oh! Ricardo said, like if time had not passed.

Get up, m'ijo! Say hello to your father, Mamá said.

Fernando knew we left Hato Mayor because I was afraid of his father.

You heard tu abuela, Ricardo said.

So, Fernando walked to stand in front of me. He was trying to protect me from his father.

Tell me, would he have done that if I had been a bad mother?

Papá stood near us, his bat leaning on a tree close by.

¿Él no habla español? Ricardo joked. You speeky English only?

Leave him alone, Ricardo, I said.

Ricardo went to hug him, but Fernando stepped back.

You're going to disrespect your father like that? Ricardo said and lifted his hand like he was going to hit him.

Then I stood in front of Fernando. Ricardo pushed me to the ground. You should have seen the terror in Fernando's eyes.

Ricardo laughed, like it was all a joke.

Qué maricón, he said.

Ay, Dios mío. I closed my eyes, afraid to look.

Fernando grabbed the neck of his father.

Nooo! I screamed. Fernando looked stronger than his father, but he was just a boy. Very fast, Ricardo had Fernando on his back. I jumped on Ricardo. I punched and kicked him.

He laughed.

Basta! Papá yelled and took his bat.

Thank God Ricardo respects Papá.

Fernando started to cried. In Hato Mayor, men can't cry in public. It was like he proved what his father said to him.

Ricardo laughed, said goodbye to my parents. I'll be back another day, he said.

Mamá waited until Papá left to yell at me. ¡Pendeja! You left Ricardo. You stole his son from him. And you're raising him like a mamagüevo? She slapped me.

She hit me in front of my son, like she hit Ángela in front of me.

This is your fault, she said. You and Ángela did not come out like me. You're both pendejas.

I never returned back to that house.

Did Mamá call me after? Never. We call her. We send money to her.

Yes, of course we have to do it, if not everybody will talk. You know, everybody. Because she's my mother and she has nobody but us.

What I'm trying to say is . . . I'm a different mother. With Fernando I tried to find him. I never gave up. Never. It's the mother's job to try with the children. My mother never tried. And with the time, she never changed. I changed. People say it's not possible to change, but I changed.

Do I regret? What do you mean? Am I sorry for what I did? For trying to keep Fernando safe? No, I don't regret. I was a good mother. I did everything I knew. But . . . but . . . I regret . . . How do I say? I never asked Fernando about his life. I don't know why. Maybe I didn't want to know. Of course, I asked myself if he had a girlfriend. I always said, Be careful in the streets. Be careful with the girls. I bought him a box of condoms and put it in the gaveta with his socks. Yes, really! I can be moderna too. But he never used them, so I thought maybe he was slow. He was always so silent. I thought he was quiet like Papá, who almost never talks. So I didn't ask.

When we were children, Mamá didn't talk to me or ask my opinions. She never did like Ángela does with the children who asks, Yadiresela, how did that make you feel? Ha! Mamá never cared about that. She told me what to do y ya.

And if I said something, Mamá got angry and said, Stop inventando. And now I see how Ángela says to Yadiresela to write down all the ideas on a paper! Ángela wants to listen to everything the children think. *Pfft!* Things are very different now.

Like Mercedes Sosa sings, todo cambia.

Todo, except Mamá.

You know, one time La Profesora in La Escuelita asked us to make a picture from when we were children. I said, It was very nice. We were happy.

Lulú looked to me surprised because she had asked me many times if I remember a moment when Mamá was good to me, and I said no. The good things in Hato Mayor were the chinolas, the agua de coco, the music that played all the day in the houses, the jokes around the fire when the batatas cooked. But one good thing about Mamá? No. I could not remember one time she was sweet to me. Isn't that strange?

You know what I regret? I didn't defend Fernando that day with Mamá. Ricardo was an animal. But Mamá, the way she talked to us—I am too humiliated to repeat. Mamá was so angry with me for treating Ricardo with disrespect. Mamá insulted us:

Me, una malcriada.

Fernando, un mamagüevo.

I went to stay with a cousin in San Pedro de Macorís until we could take the plane to New York. We didn't even say goodbye.

Me? No, it doesn't hurt me. I don't think about the past. I know how Mamá is. She is never going to change. Punto final.

That's why I get angry with Ángela, because she always wants to remind me of what happened when we were children. This happened, that happened, Mamá did this, Mamá did that. Ay! Why talk that now? We can't change it. Déjalo.

But she says, We must talk or else we will get sick. To hold things inside makes us sick. But what am I going to do? I grew up different. If we don't talk about something, it goes away.

Yes, it disappears. How?

That's true. I *am* talking about the past to you now.

Yes, maybe it hurts a little. Coñazo. But I don't want to hurt.

But listen. This is what I wanted to tell you today. Look, look at this. Like my life needs more problems. The management gave me this paper. Read it. They say if I don't pay the rent I owe, they will throw me out of the building.

I told you the management has no feelings.

You have another Kleenex?

Ay, I am sorry. I can't talk more. If it's OK with you, I want to go home.

OK. Thank you.

THIRTY (30) DAY
NOTICE TO TERMINATE

DATE: Year of 2009

TO: Cara Romero (Tenant)

CURRENT PREMISES: GENTRIFIED RENT-STABILIZED BUILDING, INC.
The Management That Has No Feelings,
on Behalf of the Landlord
Little Dominican Republic, NYC

PLEASE TAKE NOTICE: That the Landlord hereby elects to terminate your tenancy of your subsidized housing that you have had for over ten, fifteen, twenty years? Now that area codes 10032/33 have become desirable and one of the most affordable premises in New York City for downtownites, the Landlord will commence Summary Proceedings under the statute to remove you if you do not remove yourself from the apartment one month (30 days) from this dated document. We do not recognize that said premises are a place you have called home for decades, where your extended friends and family live. Your Lease Agreement states Owner shall have the exclusive right to terminate this Licensee Agreement at any time for any reason or for no reason on thirty (30) day notice.

LANDLORD: GENTRIFYING LEASING
PROPERTIES, INC.
BY: The Management That Has No Feelings
DATE: After broken windows were repaired, graffiti was
removed, and the Everything Store was replaced by the
White People Café.

SESSION TEN

I know, I am early today. I woke up thinking about everything you told me when you called, and I am so sorry that you were worried about me last week. Thinking about the past and then the present problems. Too much. Like the Americans say, when it rains it pours. But talking to you clarified many things for me.

You were right, I had to find a way to make things correct with Ángela. If there is one person in the position to help me in this moment, it is her.

Like they say, la interesada has to put on the batteries. So I watched Channel 15 every minute and finally saw Ángela in the lobby coming home from work. She was wearing her moño profesional, and when she is like this she has a difficult character. But I was ready. I put on the lipstick, took the stairs to the sixth floor, where she lives, and waited for her to get off the elevator. Qué susto I gave her, santo Dios. She was tired. She had bags under her eyes. Taking care of the children without my help is too much for Ángela. For sure, she was drowning.

When she saw me, she said, Not today, Cara, and she tried to walk away from me. But I grabbed her arm. I didn't want to make a show in the hallway, but it was my only opportunity to talk.

Don't be like that, I said.

I want to go home, she said.

Is this about Julio? Por Dios, Ángela. He doesn't even

remember that I yelled to him a little bit. Did you want me
to let him destroy the house?

Cara, you'll never understand.

You give too much mind to things, I said. This is the
problem. Every little thing is a big thing with you.

Let me go, please. The children are waiting for me.

I come with you, I said. I need you to help with something.

Of course you do! You always need something, she said.

I was shocked. Me? I never need nothing. Yes, sometimes
I need help with the burocracia; who doesn't? But many
things I do by myself. You know this about me, right?

I told her if I am such a big burden, then I will never
bother her again. I told you that Ángela wanted me to disappear, right? You see, family is a burden to her. For me, taking
care of the children is a pleasure—but she needs to understand
that I don't want them to grow up like animals. It's incredible
to me that for her to help me—¡le pesa! It's like I am asking
her to carry a bag full of shit.

I told her, Don't worry, when you leave to Long Island
you will never have to see me again.

I asked her for so little in my life. When Fernando left
me, she didn't cry for me. You know what she said? She said,
Do better. What kind of expression is that? I am sure it is
from one of her books. Do better. Do better. I work more
than every other person I know. I do best. More best than
best. I would not be surprised if she, like Lulú's daughter
Antonia, is in the therapy and spits on our mother. And now
spits on me. Ángela has no idea the sacrifices I did. No idea.
Not only for her, but her children too. Ask Lulú, who sometimes asks me to go dancing with her in El Deportivo, but I

always say no. Why? Because Ángela, who works very hard all week, wants to go out on a date night with Hernán every Friday. Ha! Even to have fun and make the love there is the schedule. So I stay home and watch the children. It's a pleasure for me, but still, Ángela, cuánto me jode.

Like I said, I didn't want to make a show in the building. I wanted peace with Ángela. But Ángela screamed. No words. Just screamed. So we made a show. Everybody appeared and watched. Lulú, Tita, La Vieja Caridad, Hernán, Yadiresela, Milagros, Julio, Glendaliz, the blanquito from the fifth floor, everybody rushed from upstairs and downstairs to see the show. And Ángela does not like to make a show. She gets mortified when people see her true character. But it was too late. She was encendía—and she had a lot to say.

Like what? Ha!

She said I make her crazy!

She said she was tired of being responsible for me. That because of me she has been stuck in Washington Heights living in a tiny apartment with three children, sharing one bathroom. In Hato Mayor, her apartment would be a big palacio.

I told her it's better to stay in Washington Heights and save her money, but for the record I never told her she couldn't leave. I told her why did she want to move to so far away to a place with strange people? I thought she was staying for Hernán, who worked in the hospital. But now me lo saca en cara that she stayed for me? ¡No me jodas! ¡Coñazo!

She said she was tired of managing all my documents. Like why has it taken me five years to file for citizenship? She said without citizenship I don't qualify for all the benefits. She said she's tired of worrying about what will happen to me if I don't find a job. Then she said that I never tell her anything.

Like what?

Like the surgery! How do you think that makes me feel, she said. If something happens to you, you are my responsibility.

You knew about the surgery? I asked her.

I know everything about you! she said.

I was shocked. Pero shocked.

So, I said, OK, OK, I declare you free. Go! You have no more obligation to me. You're free from me.

I walked away, started to take the stairs to my apartment. Everybody was there to get the chisme of the hermanas Romero.

Ángela followed me. When Hernán tried to stop her, she pushed him away.

Cara, I don't want to lose you. I just want you to stop.

Stop what? I asked her.

Stop being like Mamá. You can't help yourself. Always with the insults and negativity.

What are you talking about?

Cara, you always say to me: Ángela you're so flaca. Ángela you're so American. Ángela you're not maternal. Do you know how I felt seeing how easy you make Yadiresela stop crying? I did everything and she didn't stop crying. And then you picked her up, y mira, immediately she stopped. I am maternal! I am a mother too! And you attack everything I do like you were such a good mother, like you didn't push Fernando away. I remember how he got so anxious and tense when he heard you opening the door. You know what he said to me? Tía, I can't relax around Mami. Imagine that.

Imagine what that must feel like to be home and never be able to relax. Qué horror. And I always defended you. I said, Be patient with her. I told him how hard our mother was on us. But coño, Cara, you were relentless with him.

Because I loved him!

You have to learn another way to love, she said. You have to.

What do you mean?

You can start by apologizing, and meaning it, she said.

For what?

For scaring Julio, to start. For doing something I explicitly asked you not to do.

But he was—

Cara, just say you are sorry, Lulú said. She was standing there, seeing everything.

But—But—I would never hurt Julio. Never, I said to both of them.

Cara, you are my sister and I need you, Ángela said.

You need me? When she said this, ay, my chest. Ha! Vindication. She needs me. I told you she needed me.

Of course I need you. My children need you, Ángela said. But I want my children to grow up feeling safe in the house. To know that they can tell me anything. I want them to look to my face and see what I see in them: Possibility. Beauty. Intelligence. We cannot be like Mamá. We cannot. We have to change. If you want to be near my children, Cara, you have to change, or we will be stuck here forever. Do it for Yadiresela. Do it for Fernando. Maybe, if you change, he will come back. Have you ever thought about that?

Ángela's eyes were full of water. I tell you, she never cries. She holds it inside. I let it out. That is how we've been all our lives. Even when my mother almost killed her, she held it inside, and that only infuriated my mother more.

I'm sorry, I said. We could've done things differently.

Ángela's tears came, fast and loud. It looked like she was having a heart attack. She pressed one hand on her chest like it hurt. The other hand grabbed my shoulder.

Breathe with me, I said. I took long, deep breaths until Ángela started breathing with me. This I learned from La Vieja Caridad, who always reminds me of the power of the breath.

Breathe in belly.

Breathe in chest.

Breathe out. It helps.

You're OK, I said. I pulled her into my arms and held her tight like I know how to do. Her tears everywhere, my shirt and neck. You can imagine my fountain too.

Here, Lulú said, giving us Kleenex.

Hernán told everybody that the show was finished.

And it was strange, but I started to laugh. But laugh! And then she laughed too. So loud and hard. It felt like all the windows and doors were opened inside of us.

I tell you: Ángela se desahogó. In front of everybody.

Yes, I need some water because today I have to tell you many things.

OK, last week, after I left here, I received an email from Alicia the Psychic. She said, Carabonita, the time has arrived. I looked in my calendar, and she remembered the date! She had performed the Galactic Triangulum Magnetization ritual that she promised me to do if I sent her $79. I know I said I do not send her the money, but she made less the price especially for me. Usually it's $159. But for me half. It was necessary to guarantee my fortune. And she did not lie, because in the email she told me that she had received three very clear visions for me.

One was of me walking down the street and holding money in my hand.

Two was of me in a table full of people and I was holding a check with my name for $14,000.

Three was of me sitting by the water with someone. And in the vision, I say: I have never felt so happy like I am now.

She said, Carabonita, pay attention. In the next three weeks you will receive your fortune. Say yes to success! Say yes to wealth beyond your wildest dreams! Say yes to happiness!

If I needed to call her for further explanation it was $4.99 for the first minute and $0.99 for each additional minute. But do not worry, I will not call. Mission number one is to save my apartment. For this I need $3,091, plus my rent for next month. So every penny I can save, I save. Ángela and Hernán told me, if necessary, they can get a small loan so I do not lose the apartment. But I do not have money to pay the loan, so I need to find a real solution. The good news is that I was right to trust in Alicia the Psychic because, just like her vision, I was walking down the street and, yes, I was holding dollars.

Let me explain.

This weekend I went to the post office with Lulú to mail my application for my papers to become a citizen and take the official exam. Yes, I know, finally I do this because I do not want Ángela to worry about me. It is also important because Ángela is correct, we have to be extra careful. With the computers, they catch everybody.

For example, look what happened to Doña Altagracia. She went to visit the daughter and the grandchildren and stayed only for a few months in the Dominican Republic. When she returned, she went to the office of the government to continue the benefits. The man in the office asked for a photo identification. Doña Altagracia showed her passport. Big mistake. He reported that she went out of the country while she was collecting the benefits, and now they make her pay for the three months she received the cupones. Can you believe that? Look, Doña Altagracia worked in the factory until she was seventy years old. Seventy! In this point of her life, it is better than any pill for her to be around people who love her and will take care of her. The winter is difficult for old people. It's medicina to feel the heat of that sun. I don't know. Does the government prefer that she gets sick and dies from loneliness? Ends up sola in a bed in some facility?

And then I ask myself why would the man in the government office report her? What kind of people are these? He can choose to not look to the trips in the passport. If that was my job, I would be blind to all the old people, so they can live their last days with less stress. But no. He stopped Doña Altagracia's benefits, and she has to pay three months of cupones from the time she was outside the country. Like somebody who qualifies for the benefits has the money to pay that bill.

Before computers, people had more flexibility. Now we have to be very careful. The computers know everything about us. In the airport they scan the eyes and the fingers y quién sabe what else. Everything is documented.

So yes, I sent the application, and I made an appointment to do the civic exam. So it's official. I'm going to become American. Now when we drink wine, Lulú practices with me the exam for the citizenship because there is one hundred questions. One hundred! I only have to know ten, but they don't tell you what ten. Lulú said that I only need to get six correct.

It's easy, she said. Common sense. Any person who can count one, two, three can pass. But tell me you, what is common sense about a question like this? I have the book here, listen:

What is the rule of law?

1. Everyone must follow the law.
2. Leaders must obey the law.
3. The government must obey the law.
4. No one is above the law.

Do you know the answer? You have to think about it, yes or no? It's not so common sense, the way Lulú told me.

Lulú gets frustrated with me. She is like, Cara, just answer the questions!

I told her I read the Constitution: We the people. Think about it. We the people. Who are these people? It's not me. It's not you. The day we become inconvenient, this government will find a way to throw us out.

Maybe El Obama is different. I am optimista. When he says, this is *our* moment, this is *our* time, I think maybe because he is the son of an immigrant he understands the situation. Honestamente, when he became the president I felt it right here, on my chest. I felt light, less scared of the future for us. So it's easier to breathe now. Maybe he will stop the killing of immigrants at the border.

Lulú says gracias a Dios the test is multiple choice because with my mouth I would never get my papers. Honestly, applying for the citizenship feels a little bit like treason. It will not be easy to say I am American, because when someone says American they don't imagine me.

Why? You know why? Because I have an accent. I look dominicana. Do you feel American?

Yes. Interesting.

I don't know, I think to get the papers is like marrying someone who has no feelings for me. But also sometimes getting married has benefits.

Who knows? If God wants it, I am going to be American.

So, yes, I will study hard to pass the test. I don't want to be like my neighbor Fedora, who took the exam three times. Three! But, between you and me, Fedora is not so intelligent. You know why I say this? She did not vote for El Obama. When I discovered this, I decided to treat her nice—we exchange some dishes—but I understand she is different than me.

With the papers I can vote. To me this is important because there are many people like Fedora who make the wrong choice. With the papers, if Mamá dies—I am not trying to curse her with this thought, but if she does happen to die—maybe I can solicit the papers for Papá so that he can come to live with us and his grandchildren. But the biggest benefit, and this I'm sure you know already, is that I qualify for a job with the government. So someday I can be like you. What do you think about that? Are you laughing at me? Ah, you're smiling because I am smiling. Ha! But it's true, right? All I need is a high school diploma.

My point is that when I went to mail the application with Lulú I told her about Alicia the Psychic and her visions. Of course, Lulú did not trust. She said, If you are that lucky and that robot is real, then prove it to me.

She was not being very nice, but when she is not happy, I am careful and try not to push the wrong buttons. Learn this from me: When someone is desperate and miserable like Lulú, because every day she gets more bad news about Adonis, they are not generous with the other people. It's true that I also have problems, but Lulú has more big problems than me. In the bodega I bought the lotto card that you have to scratch. You win or lose in an instant. I thought of something Walter Mercado told me. Yes, I know he told everybody. But he said, Leave no space for negativity. Focus on the positive. Focus on love. Focus on what is possible. And then, if you do that, the good things will fill your life and there will be no space for the bad things.

I say this to you because you are young and have no problems. At your age everything is possible. But for me, even if a lot of terrible things are happening to me right now, if I remember to breathe deep, I don't feel lost. So I breathe. And I breathe. And I scratched the lotto card believing that Alicia the Psychic was doing the Galactical Magnetization so that I could secure my fortune.

And I won $25!

It's true I had to spend $5 for the lotto card, but this is what is interesting about the story: the cashier only had dollar bills and gave me $25. I left the store holding the dollars, so happy to prove Lulú was wrong. And then I saw myself in the reflection of the glass of the store and there was the vision of Alicia the Psychic. Me, holding money in my hand in the street.

No, don't worry, I will not buy any more of those cards.

They are dangerous for a person without money. But with all the crazy in my life, it was fun to play the lotto. Yes, yes, I understand it's not a permanent solution.

So let's talk about the jobs you recommended to me. They are very good recommendations and I have been thinking about them. For example, the security job you showed me weeks ago. I think I would be happy to do the class to get my certification. I think I can be good for detecting the intruders. For sure, nobody suspicious could get past me. I could monitor the students in the entrance of the school and make sure they have permission to leave. I can watch them when they eat lunch. I can receive the packages and inspect them. But to answer the phone? No. All the jobs you share with me that require the phone, I cannot do. I detest to talk on the phone in English. I don't know why, but when I am on the phone I understand only half of what the people say. La Vieja Caridad told me that this happens because I listen to people using my nose and my eyes. That's interesting, no?

But I trust what she says. I learn many things from La Vieja Caridad. The other day when she came to my apartment to eat we saw a documentary about whales, the ones that kill the humans. But what I learned is that everybody believes these whales are killers, but in all of the history that we know, only four humans have been killed by these whales. Four. And all of the humans that have died like this, it was because the whales were in captivity. Wouldn't you want to kill someone that puts you in a cage when your nature is to be free in the big ocean? Imagine to not have the space to swim. Imagine to be separated from your family.

But in this documentary, the grandmother, who is also the leader of all the whales, died. They don't know how old she was. Maybe seventy-five years old. Maybe she was more than one hundred years old, but the scientists were following this old whale for forty years. Can you believe that? And when they lost the whale in the ocean, the scientists could not even talk because they cried so much. Forty years devoted to following this whale all over the Pacific. The money they spent on the robots, the cameras, the ships, looking for this whale with their binoculars. It's incredible. It made me think of Fernando and how I still wait for him. How I look for him on Channel 15, praying that he will visit me.

But this is interesting too: The boys in the whale family struggle to survive without their mothers. All whales need their mother to eat, but boys more. When the mother dies, the boy whales are three times more likely to die in one year. One year! It's not a surprise that it is the grandmother that makes sure that every whale in the family eats. That they prove their value after la menopausia. Because not having to make babies makes them focus on taking care of the community. Which tells me that women of a certain age are more valuable to the community. Isn't it incredible?

Ah, yes, so you believe that women who don't have babies are valuable too. Ha! Perhaps you are right about this. I see how you are making me think.

This is why I like to spend time with La Vieja Caridad, because she makes me not scared to be old.

The day I saw this documentary with La Vieja Caridad, I smelled the cancer again.

I know the answer, but I asked her again. Did you check the blood to see if you are OK?

She said, Don't worry about me. I've done everything I've ever wanted to do. Cara, we must not wait to live the life we want. Find a way to be present with the people you love.

Ya tú sabes, I have told you enough for today.

APPLICATION FOR NATURALIZATION

Department of Homeland Security
U.S. Citizenship Services

Part 7. Biographic information

1. Ethnicity (Select only one box)

   ☑ Hispanic or Latino ☐ Not Hispanic or Latino

2. Race (Select all applicable boxes)

   ☑ White ☑ Asian ☑ Black or African American
   ☑ American Indian or Alaska Native

Citizen Test:

14.B. Have you ever been involved in any way with torture?

I mean, if you ask my son he say that I tortured him. He didn't like when I looked in his hair, and put crema on the cheeks, but they very dry, his skin. Oh, and if I looked in his drawers because I wanted to fix the clothes, he became angry. But what he hides? Stop looking to me, he would say. But who else was I to look at?

14.C. Have you ever been involved in any way with killing, or trying to kill, someone?

No. Never.

14.D. Have you ever been involved in any way with badly hurting, or trying to hurt a person on purpose?

What is this test trying to say about me? I never want to hurt anybody. I am not like Mamá, who make me kneel on rice for looking at her the wrong way.

14.E. Have you ever been involved in any way with forcing, or trying to force, someone to have any kind of sexual contact or relations?

Now how many people answer this question honestly? I see in the news many people in this country—even the priests do bad things and they get the papers.

17. Were you ever a part of any group, or did you ever help any group, unit, or organization that used a weapon against any person or threatened to do so?

One time we put needles on the doll to stop one of the jefes at the factory from doing bad things. Ha! Did it work—he never walked straight again.

30.A. Have you ever been a habitual drunkard?

A few glasses of wine with Lulú. It's good for the health. The doctors say seven drinks a week is a problem. But two glasses of wine for me, I feel nothing. What do you think?

30.B. Have you ever been a prostitute or procured anyone for prostitution?

Like if somebody buy me a present for sex? Bueno . . .

30.G. Have you ever gambled illegally or received income from illegal gambling?

I sometimes play números at the bodega.

48. If the law requires it, are you willing to bear arms on behalf of the United States?

Against who?

Grand Opening!

MAKE ME OVER

Salón y Laundry
2123 Second Avenue
El Barrio, NY 10029

Con mucho amor
Alexis the Pisces
20% Off on first
haircut

SESSION TWELVE

I have so much to tell you. You won't believe what happened this week. So many good things. And so many sad things. But life is like this. I can't believe this is the last time we meet together.

First, I want to tell you I am sorry I didn't come to the session last week. You know me. I never take the day off. Even with the pain of the surgery I came to the sessions. Ay, Dios mío, when I tell you what happened you will understand.

Please tell me you did not report my absence. No? Ah, OK. Good. You did the right thing because I need that check.

When you called I couldn't talk too much because I was very busy. I wanted to call you back, but I was making arrangements for La Vieja Caridad.

It's very sad. La Vieja Caridad murió in her sleep. The day was beautiful so I took Fidel to a long walk in the park because like babies that need to socialize for emotional intelligence, dogs need to play with other dogs. When I returned, I prepared the toast and the café con leche for La Vieja Caridad and took it to the room, but she was gone. Not cold, but no breath.

This nine days ago.

Yes, I am sorry too. Every day at 4:45 in the afternoon I still wait for La Vieja Caridad to call. I feel the emptiness of La Vieja Caridad. Could you imagine? For over two years, she ate in my apartment almost every day.

But it is better she died in her sleep. La Vieja Caridad was very independent. She said, Cara, the moment you see I can't defend myself, do me a favor: get a wheelchair, take me to a cliff, and push me off.

Of course, I would never agree to that, but she was talking in serious.

She was lucky because she died the way she wanted. Until the very end she had all her faculties. She never let me forget when I made a mistake with a mandao. She knew everybody's phone number from memory. Apart of the meals I prepared and the cleaning I did for her, she did everything herself.

When I found her, she was wearing the dark blue pajamas I buy her for Christmas many years ago. It made her look elegant. I made her good for the photo. I put the extra pillow behind the head. I closed the mouth. Took the almond oil on the table next to the bed and rubbed it on the forehead, around the face, in the arms and the chest. She didn't like it when the skin look like ceniza. I combed her short canas, smoothing the curls so they looked more beautiful. I took some lipstick from my purse and put a little on the cheeks for color. I put a little on her lips, but just a little, because La Vieja Caridad liked to be natural, all the time.

The room did not smell like death yet. I think La Vieja Caridad died in peace. Of course, Fidel jumped in the bed and licked her face and the hands. I tried to stop him, but then I thought, this would make La Vieja Caridad happy. She shared the spoon with Fidel.

It was good that La Vieja Caridad left everything in order. All the necessary phone numbers on the door of the refrigerator. All the papers in the folder inside a tin box that she had from when she first moved into the building sixty years

ago. Sixty! In the folder there was the paper that says, Do
Not Resuscitate. A paper with the numbers of all the doctors. The receipt for the funeral arrangements. Everything
was prepared and paid.

La Vieja Caridad stopped talking to her family many
years ago. Her sister was religious and didn't approve that La
Vieja Caridad lived with the friend instead of a husband. She
didn't know her nieces and nephews and also the children of
the nieces and nephews. How tragic. Except one of them,
who I assumed was going to inherit everything of La Vieja
Caridad's life. They wrote letters to each other two or three
times a year.

I asked La Vieja Caridad many times if losing the connection to her family to live a different life valió la pena. She
said, Who wants to live in a lie? Freedom is being able to live
your truth without having to apologize for it.

Her apartment was full of things from the ninety years of
life. Furniture more old than me. Everything in great condition. She knew how to take care of things. The walls were
full of the art from the many trips to different countries. I
had already told her which one was my favorite and she said
when the time came I could have it. It was from las Indias.
That's right! She traveled far away. I could not even imagine
being in the plane for such a long time.

The painting is blue and gold, the same color of the sea.
She told me the story of the painting about a boy and a tree.
The boy was hungry and he wanted to eat, so the tree gave
him the fruit. But when the stomach was full, the boy became
cold, so the tree gave him the branches so he could build the
house. But once he had the house the boy wanted to travel
and he went to the tree and asked if he could have the trunk

of the tree to build a boat, but the tree said, No y no y no. I am sorry. Without my trunk I cannot give you fruits and branches. I want to stay alive so I can have more to give to you in the future. Pero toma, the tree said and gave the boy some seeds so he could plant another tree to build the boat and travel.

Isn't that a good story? Ha!

But anyways, I called the ambulance, and when I was waiting for them, I boiled canela so the apartment did not smell bad. I called the number of the niece of La Vieja Caridad that I found on the refrigerator and left a message. I called Lulú, Ángela, Tita, and Glendaliz so they understood what was happening.

I swept the apartment. I cleaned the dust from the shelves. I wiped the sink. It was very strange to see her in the bed and know she was gone. When the ambulance arrived, Glendaliz said she could wait for the funeral people. So I went home. The smell of dying was going to come and it would be too much for me.

When I arrived to my apartment I sat on the table next to the window, looked to the view of the bridge, and cried. How can I explain? Suddenly, I remembered the sensation I had when I lost my job in the factory: a profound sensation of empty.

It was different than when Fernando left because I always think that one day I will see him again. It was different than when I left Hato Mayor because I was running away from that. La Vieja Caridad was gone forever. My job was gone forever.

It felt like I lost a part of me. But I mean physically lost a part of me. Could you imagine after twenty-five years to suddenly stop the routine of going to work? Every day, Iván and his van picked us up on the corner and took us to the factory across the George Washington Bridge. Rain, snow, cold, hot. Every day we would get into the small van carrying our lunches, checking in with each other. Every day crossing the bridge I saw the sun come out of the darkness. Few people in the world get to see that view.

When I was working in la factoría I didn't want Friday to come. For me it was the most sad day of the week. Especially after Fernando was gone. Always I asked for overtime. I did not like to sit in my apartment. If someone asked me for help, I said yes to stay busy. So when they took away my job, I felt empty.

Sometimes I stayed in the bed in the darkness, waiting for the sun to come in, and the clock tick and tick and the days were so long. It was more like a torture in the winter. There were no birds singing. No children outside playing. No music in the streets. If it wasn't for Lulú, who came every morning at the same time to have un café, I don't know if I would have left the bed.

For me, it's better to work. I tell you this because I need something good to happen with a job and even if this is my last day with you, I hope you will not forget about me.

So yes, I was very sad the day La Vieja Caridad died. I felt the world come on top of me. I thought about Ángela and Hernán leaving me to go to Long Island. And now La Vieja Caridad was gone. And Fernando, will he ever return to me? Slowly, everybody was leaving.

I cried. But I did not cry alone that night. In truth, many

people knew and loved La Vieja Caridad because she was the last of the viejas in the building. Even Fernando loved her because she always carried candy in her bag for the children.

Without planning, we all ate dinner together to remember her. I cooked for everybody that wanted to come. I made the chicken, the ribs, the moro with habichuelas negras, the plátanos, and the salad of aguacate.

Hernán brought two bottles of wine. I made the table more big so we could all sit together. Ángela came early to help to organize the chairs. We never know who will appear, so it's good to be ready. And, let me tell you, you will be proud of me and my behavior management with the children. When Julio took the chicken and ran around the house doing a mess, I did not yell or grab him so he could behave. I said, in a very calm way, Julio, food is for eating. Please come to the table. I did!

Of course, he did not pay attention to what I said, because no behavior management will change his character, but I could see that Ángela was impressed by me. That's when I realized that another one of the visions of Alicia the Psychic came true. Remember? She saw me in a table full of people and I was holding a check. At that moment, there was no check, but she was right about the table and the people. And this made me think that my fortune was coming.

When La Vieja Caridad died, I had many strange dreams. In one of them I was waiting for the train and I saw a woman, much more young than me. She had a stroller that was going to fall into the tracks, and there was a baby in there. She was falling asleep and not paying attention. So when the train came to us, I grabbed the stroller and pulled it back. When I saw the woman's face, it was me. A more young me. From when I came to New York with $10 and Fernando on my hip. He was all the time on my hip. And he was heavy. I was alone with no family to hold him so I could rest.

I say this like if my mother ever helped with Fernando when I was still back home. She had three children, but she didn't like having us. This was clear.

If my mother had been born in New York I think she would've lived like La Vieja Caridad, free from children, but, instead of a dog, my mother would've had birds. In Hato Mayor she fed many birds. One time I saw Mamá dancing to a song by herself, and when she saw me, she stopped. I don't know why she had to hide to be happy from us. I think she loved my father. He was a basket that could hold water. But she didn't choose him. When she had fourteen years he took her to his house and she never left. Same story with her mother. That's how things were done.

Mamá did very little for me. But one day she gave me a piece of paper with a New York address and said, If you want, you can go there.

You ever heard the expression, When you're hungry, no bread is too hard to eat?

You and I know nothing is free. I left home with my skin pegá to my bones. A small bag filled with a few things. Fernando close to my chest. I ate the stale bread and focused on finding work and making money. I didn't want to depend on no man for the ceiling over my head or the food I eat. Punto final.

We first lived in a room in a building a few blocks from

here. The address was from a cousin who had made the travel, years before. I paid $40 a week. The lady who owned the apartment gave the bed, the sheets, the towels, and the use of the kitchen for one hour a day. I had secured the job in the factory, and a place for Fernando in the day care nearby. I made relations fast with another mother—for $10 a week, she took Fernando to the day care so I could take the van going to the factory.

Look, only a mother knows what a mother does. After working I would take care of Fernando's needs. Including pumping the milk for four years. I gave him the breast for four years, even if it emptied me. Leche de oro. Never did he get sick on me. It also kept Fernando close to me and healthy.

In that time, we were alone together. My body maintained him calentito in the winter when we had no heat. He needed me to survive. When I hear the words in the English coming from his mouth, I thought maybe he could have a more easy life because people would listen to him. This helped me to survive.

So, yes, I was a good mother to Fernando, but I can now see that I was also this mother in the dream, young, afraid, alone, falling asleep near the tracks of the train.

The super wanted all the furniture out of La Vieja Caridad's apartment by the first of the month, so I only had a few days. That is why I couldn't come to see you. La Vieja Caridad's niece lives in Europe, so she could not help me. I spent many hours separating the things that La Vieja Caridad sold to the Next Life Furniture Store before she died. I had to wait for them to pick it up. Then, between all of us, we took the table, the painting, the clock. All the things that were left.

And then when I looked through La Vieja Caridad's papers inside the tin box, I found a letter to me. Yes, she left me a letter. Signed. Official. Incredible.

Do you understand what I am trying to tell you? Alicia the Psychic was right. I was holding the money on the street from the lotto. I was around the table with the people. And then I discovered that a check of $5,600 was coming to me from La Vieja Caridad.

Can you believe it?

You do? You believe in Alicia the Psychic too?

Oh, you believe in *me*? Ha! You are making me very emotional. Of course, you are right. I took good care of La Vieja Caridad. But I never did anything for La Vieja Caridad for money. Never.

Now you understand why I couldn't come to the last session. I felt like the boy in the painting who got the fruit and the branches, but I must be careful to want too much in this life. This is the lesson. We must appreciate what we have.

So, of course, I was suffering, but also surprised that La Vieja Caridad thought of me. But around Lulú, I could not talk about my luck, because Lulú was not so lucky like me.

I know, I am not just lucky. You are very good to remind me of this. I work hard all the time. You are right I must take some credit for this. But it's crazy because Lulú was the one that liked to show off how everything was so good in her life. And this was true. For many years Lulú got many presents from her son. A new mattress, a new knife to cook, a set of good pots. He was generous with her. This made her happy. But in the past two months, the only thing her son Adonis gave her is more worry. This proves that the more money you make, the more problems you make. And now, Adonis, Patricia, and the babies moved into Lulú's apartment. And, of course, now Lulú is cooking, cleaning, and taking care of four people.

Ay, pobrecita Lulú. You can imagine how upset she is. She is not like me. I am easy. If I have to accommodate ten people in my apartment, it's no problem. But Lulú likes to have her own room that she can close the door. She says, A leona needs her own cave. She is a Leo, so this makes sense. With the entire family inside the two-bedroom apartment, she will have no place to be alone. Only the bathroom. And they have to share that.

Then I had a great idea. Because I have money, I thought I would take Lulú to the salón of Alexis. Yes, Alexis, remember him? He sent me this card. Maybe he sent the card to everybody he knows. But also to me. Yes, it is in El Barrio—I know, so far away, but maybe he has news about Fernando. So I said to Lulú, Please come with me to this salón?

Why so far?

Ay, Lulú, do this for me. I need to fix my hair, I said. But really she needed to fix her hair. She looks abandoned. Still no faja. She is wearing a bra for the jogging. Do you understand what I am saying? For the jogging! It smashes your tetas. Not good.

Oh, you also wear the bra for the jogging every day? Really? Ha!

She looked at my hair and made a face. Imagine that. Me, who looks very good even if my life is hard like hers.

I will go with you, she said. If it was not for me . . .

You see what I mean? Even now, she makes like she is doing me a favor. But I permit her to be the way she is.

So we took the train to the train to the bus and we walked and walked and found the address: 2123 Second Avenue. A big sign, escrito a mano in the window, said, MAKE ME OVER: SALÓN Y LAUNDRY.

I looked inside and saw Alexis fixing a person's hair. The last time I saw him was eight years ago, but he was the same with the exception that his hair was rubio. He still looked like he belonged in the future.

On one side of the wall we saw the mirrors, the chairs, the shelves stocked with hair dryers and brushes. On the other side were the washing machines and the dryers. It made sense to do both at the same time.

When I opened the door, he turned to look at us. The lights so bright. Both Lulú and I could use a little sun, a little lipstick. A music of drums was playing.

Mami? Alexis recognized me immediately. He told me to wait. So we waited.

This is Fernando's friend? she said.

I could tell she had many opinions, but said nothing. In the past she would have said many things.

The client waved goodbye to Alexis. She looked good.

He asked me, What you doing around here?

You wrote to me! I said.

I showed him the card that said 20 percent discount.

Sit, sit, he said, looking closely to my ends. When was the last time you cut your hair?

I told her, Lulú said. Maybe she will listen to you.

I sat on that chair like a sack of arroz with a hole in it. I didn't recognize me in the mirror. My eyebrows were a disaster. When he brushed my hair, it was uneven. I didn't know because I always wear it up. But me too, I was a little abandoned. But not so bad as Lulú.

So one chair for Lulú, one chair for me.

I'll do both of you for the price of one, he said. What do you think?

Lulú had no money, so I said, Yes, if it is OK with you. We accept!

No, I am OK, Lulú said. I don't need.

She is so proud. But Alexis understood how to manage because he took out Lulú's pinchos without asking and said, Today we make you over.

Is this place yours? I asked.

All this is mine, Mami. Mine. Alexis waved his arms around the room. Freshly painted. Signs full of color. WASH AND DRY. SELF-SERVICE. 25 CENTS, 10-MINUTE DRYER.

Have you heard from Fernando?

Ay, Mami, you just missed him.

How can that be?

He is traveling a lot. His new job has him on a plane all the time.

Don't tell me. What job?

He works in a store on Madison Avenue. He designs the windows and makes everything look nice.

How did he learn to do that?

Fernando is very lucky for the jobs. People love him. He learns fast. In this world all you need is people to give you a chance.

Does he still live with you? I asked.

Not anymore. But we talk all the time. I will tell him to call you, Alexis said.

People say things and never do it, but I trusted Alexis the Pisces would do that.

Alexis raised the music to make a party. He had the lights that travel on the ceiling in many colors like a discoteca. Like a professional, he covered Lulú's canas, then washed my hair. Then he washed Lulú's hair and put it to dry. Then he cut my hair. He moved from Lulú to me back and forth, back and forth.

When he touched my head and combed my hair, I could feel my shoulders relax.

Do you trust me? Alexis said.

Yes, I trust, I said, letting him take care of me. He even cleaned my eyebrows.

You look so good, he kept saying to me and Lulú. In the mirror, we were changed. This is true.

Lulú was silent on the bus. On the train. When we returned to the neighborhood, I took her to the park to sit on a bench where we could see the bridge and the Hudson.

You look good, I said many times.

You must be happy, she said. Your Fernando is a success.

She smiled, but her eyes betrayed her.

But I understand her jealousy. It is difficult to be happy for others when you have many problems.

I paid for the salón. And La Vieja Caridad left me her money. And I have the big apartment to myself. So I told her she doesn't have to be that way, because I will share everything with her.

That is crazy, she said.

But I have an empty room. You can live in Fernando's room.

She looked to me, surprised.

It would be my pleasure. Stay with me, I said.

But . . .

But what? I said.

We are friends, not family. What will the people think if we live together?

Who cares what anybody thinks? I said, and surprised myself.

I am sure La Vieja Caridad was also smiling from the sky.

And that's when I recognized that the third vision came true.

I was sitting by the water and I was not alone.

Was I happy? I think so. But what is a cake without frosting?

This is my last will and testament.

Dear Cara,

I, Caridad Nilsa Guillois, being of sound mind, would like to leave you, Cara Romero, the monies earned from the sale of my estate. Please call the Next Life Furniture Store, who has agreed to purchase the art and furniture on the attached sheet. Everything has been appraised and will be purchased at a total cost of $5,600 U.S. dollars. Please contact them immediately. In exchange I ask that you care for Fidel with the same tenderness and love that you cared for me all these years. He has a few good years in him left. Thank you for being a good friend to me. If anyone asks, tell them that I died without regrets.

With love,
Caridad

SENIOR WORKFORCE PROGRAM

New York, United States
Job Training Progress Report

NAME: CARA ROMERO	DATE OF BIRTH: January 18, 1953

The present social work progress report addresses the following time period:

From: February 16, 2009	To: May 10, 2009	Number of sessions: 12

Client(s) failed to attend, or cancelled within 24 hours, on 0 occasion (s).

Objectives addressed during this period:
I met with Ms. Romero for twelve sessions. During this time, we discussed her various strengths. In her own words, Ms. Romero wants to work. She is strong, she is always prepared, she is a good organizer, she is good with children, she is good under stress, she likes to invent. She also believes she has unusual skills, like the ability to smell cancer and diabetes.

Although Ms. Romero has been unemployed for over two years, she has worked as a caretaker and support system for the elderly, children of various ages, and persons with disabilities, all who live in her building. A great storyteller, she has shared multiple examples to illustrate her ability to comfort, feed, and housekeep a substantial amount of people in challenging situations. My assessment is that Ms. Romero has performed a significant amount of unpaid labor for community members.

Do you recommend continuing the Senior Workforce Program for this client? If yes, what is the recommended frequency and estimated duration?
I strongly recommend an immediate renewal of unemployment benefits and twelve additional sessions with the Senior Workforce Program for Ms. Romero—with the option for renewal.

This extension is essential in securing Cara Romero's long-term employment.

Name: Lissette Fulana De Robertis	Date: June 05, 2009

All personal information collected is protected from unauthorized disclosure by the Senior Workforce Program. Clients have the right to access their personal information and the right to challenge the accuracy and completeness of this report.

EXTENSION OF BENEFITS

Approved_____   Denied_____

TWO MONTHS LATER

Do I interrupt you? No? Oh good. I have been wanting to stop by with Fidel to bring you some pastelitos without raisins because I don't like raisins. I fried them this morning, so they're fresh. Also, I brought you a café con leche from the restaurant because it is better and costs three times less than the ones they sell in the white people café.

Fidel is very friendly. Everywhere I go, he wants to go. Not even on the phone can I be without Fidel making noise. With La Vieja Caridad, he was not like this. But dogs are like humans. This I learned. They are different with everybody.

Yes, go ahead. I'm OK if you eat while we talk. Don't be shy about that. I promise that you have never tasted a pastelito like this. Right? It's good!

I wanted to thank you for calling and letting me know that you are still trying to fight for an extension of benefits for me. If that can happen, I appreciate it very much. With the money of La Vieja Caridad and the small loan Ángela made for me, I have been able to manage. I also have sold some cakes to friends. Patricia, because she is a good woman, pays half of my rent because Lulú lives with me and takes care of the children every day. I take care of the children more than Lulú because she has no patience, but, like I said, we manage. And thank you for taking Tita for this program. At least for a few months she does not have to work for that terrible lady.

Living together with Lulú? It's OK, yes. But Lulú spends

two hours in the bathroom. What does she do in there, I don't understand. She does not wash the dishes like me. Always a little bit of grease left. But I don't judge. We are different in this way.

Ángela? Yes, she lives in Shirley, in Long Island. No Dominicans there. Hernán drives to work in the hospital every day. It's crazy, all that driving, but on Fridays he takes me, and sometimes Lulú too, in the car with him to their house, and I will confess, don't tell Ángela because she will make me crazy saying she was right, but now with the good weather, to have a big patio to barbecue is very relaxing. In five minutes you can go to the beach. A little boring because nobody plays music, full of blanquitos, but Ángela is happy. The children are happy.

But I also want to tell you the incredible thing that happened. Remember Sabrina? You know, the girl I saw kissing with the friend in the stairs? With the Catholic uniform? On the day of the mothers, not the American one, the Dominican one, I was about to take the elevator and Sabrina and her mother were coming out. Of course, Sabrina was terrified when she saw me.

But then it was her mother that said something that shocked me.

While I was away doing my mandaos, she saw Fernando on Channel 15. He was in the lobby. Our lobby!

She said, You must be so happy to have Fernando back in your life.

Imagine my heart.

Wait. What? Where did you see him?

In the lobby!

You sure it was Fernando?

It was Fernando, she said. He was in the lobby.

You saw it on Channel 15?

Cien por ciento Fernando.

When I arrived to the apartment, I found a food delivery hanging on the door. You're not going to believe this! It was a delivery of chicken wings—¡ay! I love chicken wings!—with rice and beans, and ensalada de aguacate and tostones with the garlic on the side. All my favorites. With a note from Fernando: Mamá, Feliz Día de las Madres. Tu hijo, Fernando.

Could you imagine my heart when I saw his note? Of course, it was Alexis who told him to reach me.

It reminds me how every time I trust my sensation everything goes OK. This is why I am here today because this morning I thought about you and I felt to make you pastelitos. I didn't ask why. I just followed my sensation in my corazón and came to you. Like Walter Mercado taught me. Like Alicia the Psychic said in one of her letters: The time to be courageous is now. Like La Vieja Caridad said, Don't live with regrets. Be present. Trust yourself. That is why I am here. Talking to you, all these weeks, has been very good for me. I have learned a lot. Talking reminds me that no matter how difficult my life is, I have always found a solution to my problems. When I think about this, I am not afraid. We can do this. I can do it.

Write this down: Cara Romero is still here, entera.

ACKNOWLEDGMENTS

This book is set during the Great Recession in New York City, a time when many community members lost their jobs and weren't able to secure long-term employment. I would like to thank everyone who shared their stories about the challenges they faced trying to find steady income and raise their children.

I am grateful to my comadres and friends who read and/or listened to pages from the book and asked questions, shared articles, and offered feedback throughout the years. Thank you to everyone who volunteered to care for my son so I could carve out time to write. I am especially grateful to Armando Garcia, Carolina de Robertis, Dawn Lundy Martin, Idra Novey, Laylah Ali, Lissette J. Norman, Marlène Ramírez-Cancio, Marta Lucía Vargas, Milenna van Dijk, Nelly Rosario, and Tanya Shirazi.

To my editor, Caroline Bleeke, and agent, Dara Hyde, who lovingly read and reread many drafts. To the teams at Flatiron and Hill Nadell Literary Agency, who offered insightful notes. To Blue Mountain Center, The Lighthouse Works, and Yaddo for the gift of time and space.

To the Cruz, Gomez, and Piscitelli family for supporting my writing life in countless ways. Especially to my mother, Dania, who taught me so much about the importance of taking care of each other.

Thank you to my son, Daniel Andres Piscitelli-Cruz, for his patience and his significant editorial contributions. I love you so much!

It takes a village. Punto final.

ABOUT THE AUTHOR

ANGIE CRUZ is the author of the novels *Soledad, Let It Rain Coffee,* and *Dominicana,* which was shortlisted for the Women's Prize for Fiction and was a *Good Morning America* Book Club pick. She is a founder and the editor in chief of *Aster(ix),* a literary and arts journal, and is an associate professor of English at the University of Pittsburgh.